SOLD

ROMANCE IN NYC: DOUBLE DELIGHT
BOOK ONE

ANGEL DEVLIN

CHAPTER ONE

Tiffany

Monday evenings were 'girls' night' in our apartment in Dyker Heights, Brooklyn. All three of us worked as realtors for a Brooklyn real estate company and we worked damn hard. So Mondays were downtime, complete with pizza and beer. There was me, Kayla and Haley. Our Monday nights were for sharing stories about work and to catch up on our—currently nightmarish—love lives. None of us were having much luck on the romantic front.

"Please can we not watch a movie with a sexy leading man tonight, because I swear my pussy will combust and it won't be a pretty sight," Kayla moaned. At twenty-four, Kayla was tall and slim, with pale skin, and long wavy red hair. She was stunning but attracted to men who were dicks. She hadn't had a date for at least two weeks and it was killing her.

"That bad, huh?" I asked.

"Yeah, I might go visit Daniel. While I'm there, I can see if there are any hot men currently hanging around Long Island." Kayla's stepfather lived on Long Island. Her mother—a serial cheater—had moved on long ago and had lost touch with her daughter. Kayla hadn't stayed at Daniel Scott's much, but out of all her many stepfathers he had been the only one to be a pretty decent man and he had always said there was a room for her at his home, even after her mother's departure. She visited rarely, but felt she owed it to him to check in. Guilt from her mother screwing him out of a lot of his cash no doubt.

"Well, I have a date tomorrow night. I think this might be the one," Haley said.

Kayla and I groaned simultaneously. Haley was a born romantic and every date she had, she thought would be her Prince Charming. Instead, they ended up being the Princes of Darkness. Petite, with long, straight, dark-brown hair, and an ass a Kardashian would envy, Haley was soft spoken and quite innocent. She'd only had one lover—a long term sweetheart—and when he had left her after college she had been devastated. She had felt he was her one, and we were sure she believed that one day he would actually come back for her.

"God, dating sucks," I proclaimed. "I had another loser send me a message through the company email today."

"Ugh, creep." Kayla said with a smirk on her face.

It happened a lot at Green's Real Estate. Our photographs were on the web page under Agents, along with our direct line and email address. Usually, it was a breathy phone call asking whether I was wearing panties, but today's had been an actual email.

I brought it up on my cell. "Listen to this," I told my friends, then I began to read it out loud.

TIFFANY,

Is this really you on your photograph? I guess I'll have to find out by meeting you. Right now, I'm looking at this headshot with my ten-inch dick in my hand. I'm imagining that my other hand is fisting your shoulder-length, blond hair; dragging your head downward toward my cock. Those green eyes are wide and begging for me to open your pouting lips and fill you with my girth. Your pink lipgloss is smeared over my cock while I push myself in and out of your hot mouth. You might try to hide your breasts under that baggy top, but I can tell you have huge tits begging for release. I'll suck on your nipples and then I'm going to stick my cock between those creamy mountains and fuck them until I come all over your face; your smeared pink gloss mixed with my creamy cum.

Speak soon, H.

"OH MY FUCKING GOD, WHAT A CREEP," Haley gasped. "Did you report it?"

"Nah, I get similar things at least once a week. Don't you?"

Haley shook her head. "No. I've never had a message like that."

"She doesn't have a photo posted, does she?" Kayla reminded me. "She's the sensible one."

"Well, I replied that I found his post offensive and not to contact me again."

"Really?" Kayla asked cocking an eyebrow. "I

think it's damn hot."

"You think everything's hot today. You need to go out and get laid."

"I do. I really do." She whined.

"Okay, Haley, get the pizza ordered. Kayla, go grab some beer from the fridge while I choose a movie. One with some ugly dudes and no sex scenes whatsoever."

"I think even an old wrinkled guy with warts would do it for me right now," Kayla moaned.

"Chick flick it is." I announced.

THAT NIGHT, with my stomach satisfyingly full of pizza, and feeling sated thanks to a couple beers, I quickly changed into my shorts and camisole and climbed under my duvet. I dreamed vividly about a man with short blond hair. I met him in a bar and he was someone I had known in the past. Years had passed, and I found him hot and attractive. He felt the same. I woke just after we had shared a panty melting kiss, with the promise of meeting again. A sigh escaped me. It had seemed so real and yet was a figment of my overactive imagination. My thighs clenched together. I didn't want it to end there. Fuck it! I'd carry it on in my half-awake thoughts.

· · ·

I RETURN *to the bar and to the image of this blond-haired man. My lips back on his. His tongue invades my mouth, going deep and tangling with my own.*

"Want to get out of here?" He asks.

"Yes."

I pictured the frantic removal of clothing in his apartment and then my mind reverted to the email I received earlier. I tried to get my thoughts to take a different route, but they were relentless.

In my imagination I drop to my knees, taking the man's raging cock in my mouth. I'm so full, I have to stop myself from gagging. I cup his balls in my hand and lick around the tip of his swollen mushroom head, letting it slide in and out of my mouth. It makes a popping sound each time I let him free. He's frustrated and gripping my hair, forcing me to take him deeper in my throat. I suck hard and he groans, his pleasure evident on his face. He watches me, eyes alert as I continue to suck. He fucks my face hard until I feel his balls pull back, tightening, and then he fills me with his cum, emptying his load straight to the back of my throat. I swallow him down and lick my lips. He thanks me and wipes a thumb over my lip, smearing my pink lip gloss and droplets of his cum up my cheek.

"Beautiful." He says in a deep husky voice.

GODDAMN, I couldn't take any more of the fantasy, so I shoved my hand down my shorts. I could feel my engorged lips, slick with my juices, and I pushed one finger, then another, into my pussy. I pistoned them, imagining they were my fantasy lover's cock. It took me over the edge and I tried to be quiet—with my friends' rooms so near to my own—but I had to let out a tumultuous scream as I shuddered with my orgasm. The sound was unmistakable. I felt my cheeks flush. I pulled my legs together; the aftershocks, smaller shudders, still coming. My breath finally evened out, and I felt so relaxed, all the tension having left my body. I turned over in bed to finally try to get some sleep.

"I want whatever you're having." Kayla shouted out from the adjacent room.

Fuck! I pretended I was snoring by making loud noises as if I was innocent, but in reality my hand went back between my legs, feeling how soaked I was and how much I had dampened my shorts.

· · ·

OUR APARTMENT HAD one open-plan area with a dining table to one corner, a small kitchen to another, and a living room that faced a large balconied patio window. To the back of the room was a long corridor where at the end were our three bedrooms and two bathrooms. The main tenant, Haley, had the room with the en-suite bathroom and patio window with a balcony, and Kayla and I shared the other bathroom. Walking past, I could hear the shower running and her singing. I wasn't a morning person, preferring to have coffee and breakfast before my own shower, so this worked out just fine. I poured a coffee from the pot and took a seat at the corner table, banging my mug down on the table top. Hot coffee sloshed out of the mug, scalding my hand.

"Fuck me, that's hot."

Kayla chose that moment to walk through, rubbing her hair with a towel. "Is that what you were saying last night in your fantasies, you dirty bitch?"

I blushed. "I don't know what you're talking about."

"If that's how you want to play it." She impersonated my loud orgasm noise. "That noise came from your room last night; you might want to check out what it was."

Haley turned to us from her position on the

couch, throwing her magazine down. "There's nothing wrong with masturbating. We all do it. Christ, I'd have seized up by now if I didn't."

"Haley!" We said in tandem. It was so unusual for Haley to say anything so bluntly.

"Well it's true. My B.O.B. is my other best friend apart from you two."

We all laughed.

Haley changed the subject, obviously done with any carnal conversation. "What's everyone up to today? Anything exciting?"

"I'm showing a client around a condo at Brighton Beach." I told them.

"Oh my god, I love it out there," Haley said, her hands clasped together. "Swap me so I can go visit."

"Not a chance with the commission I'll earn if I get him to purchase."

"It's a purchase, not a rental?" Kayla qualified.

"Sure is. A steal at $3.5m."

"*Jeez.*" Haley said. "Do you think between us we could buy a brick each?"

I chuckled. "So, my schedule is to meet the client at eleven, and I have nothing else going on because I centered my whole day around trying to get Mr. Carter of Carter Property Enterprises, to part with his cash." I swallowed the rest of my coffee and snatched Kayla's pop tart out of her hand. I took a bite and walked toward the shower. "Catch you guys later."

"Thanks for waiting to listen about my day," Kayla yelled out. "And for eating my breakfast."

I WAITED for Mr. Carter to show up in the lobby of the Brighton Condominium and Club. The lobby looked like it belonged to a luxury hotel: with reception, and a concierge, on first entering; and with a waiting area, plus a bar and restaurant set further back. The building had twenty-four-hour security, a gym, pools, and private beach access. I didn't want coffee breath when I met my client, so I sucked on a mint while I watched the doorway.

Two men entered the building at once. One was middle-aged, balding, and short. The other looked like a movie-star. I bet I knew which one was my client. Sure enough, the older one walked toward me. "Could you tell me, are you Miss Harris?"

"I am." I shook his hand. "It's a pleasure to meet you, Mr. Carter."

"Oh, no, sorry, you're mistaken." The gentleman said. "I'm Mr. Carter's driver. He's waiting for you in the bar." I turned around, following the man's pointed finger and my gaze was met by steely gray eyes from the movie-star man. "If you would like to go through to meet him, I'll go wait in the car."

I was intrigued. He couldn't introduce himself? I supposed he didn't know for sure it was me. Not everyone looked up my photo like the pervert. I stood up and brushed down my peach, knee-length skirt. My heels clacked on the marble floor as I made my way over to the bar.

"Mr. Carter?" I held out my hand.

"Miss Harris." He took my hand in his, holding it a fraction too long. I noted his hands were huge, his fingers had thick digits. His skin was as smooth as the marble floor under my feet. I took in his appearance: blond hair that was slicked back and came to midway down his neck and a chin covered by a touch of pale stubble. He was a man who worked out, had a medium-build, and I would put him at six foot two. He was dressed in a sharp business suit, but lacked a tie, and his white shirt had the two top buttons undone.

"I thought we would talk first before you showed me the condo. I like to know who I'm doing business with." He stated.

"That's fine." I nodded, removing my peach jacket, as it was becoming too warm for me in the bar. I watched his eyes follow my jacket, pausing for a fraction as my pale-blue blouse gaped at the front. Sometimes my large bust was entirely frustrating. I tried to keep my jacket on wherever possible and cover the girls up, but today was too warm and I gave up. I'd just have to put up with my chest being spoken to. It wouldn't be the first time. However, Mr. Carter's gaze quickly returned to my face, and that's where it stayed throughout the rest of our conversation, which made a refreshing change.

He ordered us two mineral waters. I didn't mind. I found a lot of these successful businessmen liked to do that. Displaying their egos as they took charge.

I explained about my background with Green's.

"So you have a lot of experience with rich businessmen then?" He asked, appraising me coolly.

"I'm one of Green's main realtors in high end real estate."

"Could I ask you something personal?" His finger skimmed around the top of his glass which emitted a whistling sound.

"Sure, though whether I'll answer or not depends on the question."

"Do you have rich businessmen bothering you all the time, thinking they can buy you as well as the property?"

My eyes narrowed. "No. They've never been anything but professional. They know should they be anything less, their reputation would be tarnished. Green's is a very friendly firm and we are all looked after. I have an alarm that rings straight to the office. Should anything unexpected happen, the cops would be on their ass before they'd have a chance to feel mine up."

"Good. I'd hate to think you had to put up with that," he answered. Mr. Carter smiled at me and it changed his whole appearance. His face looked years younger. I swore his eyes looked a warmer shade of gray, and his lips parted to show a row of pearly white teeth with one canine slightly twisted at the right-hand side of his front teeth. The fact that he had this slight imperfection pleased me. He was too perfect before. Now he seemed more human, just from that one flaw.

"Are you ready for me to show you the condo now?" I asked him.

"Absolutely. Lead the way." He said.

We took the elevator up to the eighth floor and I walked us to the apartment and opened the door.

"After you." I told him.

He walked inside.

The apartment opened into a spacious hallway

which resembled a mini version of the downstairs lobby with the marble floor. There were coat hooks, a coat rack, shoe racks and a sofa. I pushed and held open a further door which led into a vast open living area. There were windows to the front and right of the apartment that all overlooked the beach. The sunshine streamed in through the windows making the room glow and showing it to its best potential. The view was nothing less than stunning.

Mr. Carter turned to me. "Amazing view."

"Yes, it's something isn't it?"

He looked at me and there was a beat of hesitation before he replied, "Quite something."

The open living area housed a large kitchen which ran from where the windows ended on the right-hand side. It was dark wood and masculine. Not to my taste, but I hoped it appealed to his. I was led to believe this was a personal purchase as opposed to a business one. Quite a few clients purchased Brighton Beach condos and stayed there in the summer, commuting from their New York apartments. I showed him the bathroom next which was large, white, and functional.

I sang the praises of the separate large shower cubicle.

"It's just a bathroom. It's fine. Show me the master bedroom please, Miss Harris."

"Of course, right this way."

I opened the master bedroom door, and he walked through first, heading straight for the large window which gave him the same fabulous view of the beach. His gaze scanned the rest of the room: a simple wooden bed and matching bedroom furniture.

"What's your opinion of this room, Miss Harris, because I find it lacking."

I squirmed under his stare. "I agree, this room is quite basic given the luxury furnishings of the rest of the property; however, that may be something you could use to negotiate on price."

"Do you know what would improve this room?" He asked, passing me and walking toward the door.

I shook my head. "I wouldn't know your own interests, but I'm sure you would be able to hire an interior designer to bring to life any vision you had."

"What would improve this room..." He hesitated before switching the lock on the bedroom door. "Would be your naked body lying on that bed." His voice lowered to a husky whisper. A whisper suited for seduction.

I reached into my pocket for my alarm.

He held up his hand.

"I'm not going to attack you, Miss Harris."

My heart thudded in my chest. "Then why did you lock the door?"

"Just a precaution, so that no staff members accidentally interrupt us."

"Accidentally interrupt what? I'm showing you a condo." I snapped.

He walked toward me and whispered in my ear.

"Well it's up to you. You can reach past me and unlock it. I won't stop you."

I sighed. By now I should have kicked him in the balls and made my escape, so why hadn't I?

"Perhaps I should introduce myself properly, Tiffany." He smirked and held out his hand. "My name is Henry Carter, but you can call me H."

My eyes widened. Fuck! That email. It was him!

"So, Tiff... if I may be so bold as to call you that. Either you can leave, or you can lie on that bed and we'll do everything from my email and more. You decide. All I can say is that I wasn't lying when I said ten inches."

I swallowed, and my mouth went dry.

Should I stay, or should I go?

CHAPTER TWO

H

Some might say I was taking a huge risk with the game I was playing, but I didn't give a fuck. When you're rich, life could become extremely monotonous. When you had seen one luxury apartment, you had seen them all. I had assistants I sent out to do my property investment shit. But I looked at Green's web page and eye-fucked the photo of the luscious Tiffany Harris. I sent her an email from a non-traceable address, wondering how she would react. I tricked her landlord into letting one of my men in as a television repairman. Dumb fuck. He hid a camera in her room instead. It's so easy to hide one these days. I watched as she finger-fucked herself last night. She shouted out the word H as she came. Tiffany wanted me. She wanted the thrill of me. From what I had been able to find out, she'd had two semi-serious boyfriends in the past. Maybe they could fuck, but they wouldn't have been able to give her what I could. There's more in my plan for Tiff, but for now she stood in the bedroom, biting her lip, while she decided on her next move. It had better be towards the bed.

Tiffany

JESUS CHRIST! Why hadn't I left yet?

I'd tell you why. Because the man that stood before me looked like sex on a stick and he wanted to do dirty things to me.

Because I hadn't been fucked in over three months.

Because I kept picturing that email and the fact that although I told the others it creeped me out, the truth was it made me cream my panties.

Then there was last night and my feverish orgasm from a fantasy that started with a dream man and finished with thoughts of that very email.

He would do all of that with me?

Fuck my mouth with that cock.

Fuck my tits with his huge dick.

My nipples hardened. My breasts strained against my bra trying to make a break for freedom.

I stared up at H. He had that smirk on his face. He thought I was going to bolt.

"This is just between us, right? No one will know what happened in this room?"

"Correct, Miss Harris."

"I think you should stick with Tiff, if we're going to fuck, H." A sly grin pulled at my lips.

I placed my purse and my jacket on the dresser in the room. Then I stood in front of H and unbuttoned my blouse. He watched; his gaze a far cry from the man who smiled at me in the bar downstairs. He was completely predatory.

I pulled my blouse down my arms and discarded it to the floor. It was very hard to find a good fitting bra when you had tits that poured out over the top and the sides of the cups. I made a note to pay extra to get a proper fitted bra in case I ever found myself in a position like this again. H growled, and his hands were on me in a flash.

"Those fucking big titties. They're more than I ever imagined while I was jerking off." He pulled the straps down on either side and pulled my bra down at the front, so my boobs broke free, bouncing against my chest.

His mouth descended onto a nipple and he attempted to cup my breast in his hand. His hand might have been large and meaty, but it was no match for my breast. "Christ, I need two hands for one tit." He dropped one hand and grabbed one of my own and held it against his crotch. He was hard as a rock and I could feel he was about to punch through his own pants if his cock wasn't freed soon. I opened the button of his suit pants and then lowered the zip. It was a struggle against the size of his erection. As his pants came down, I pulled down his boxers and that enormous cock sprang free. Holy shit! There was no way that monster was going to fit in me. I had never seen anything like it in my life. My previous lovers had been average. A bead of pre-cum glistened on the end of his shaft and I ran my finger over it.

"Taste it." He demanded.

"You wanted me to smear it with the pink gloss,

did you not?" I put the droplet on my finger and smeared it onto my lip.

He grabbed my tits and pinched my nipples hard.

"That's for not doing as I asked. I asked you to taste me. I'll decide when your mouth gets coated with my cum, not you."

Oh, he liked to be in charge. Well, I was fine with that. I was feisty in real life, but in the bedroom, I could play a part.

He squeezed the end of his dick, so another droplet appeared. "Now, taste me." He demanded once again.

I swiped the bead of pre-cum with my finger and I sucked my finger into my mouth. My finger made a popping sound when I removed it.

"How do I taste?"

"Hmmm, like citrus and salt." I said breathily. "Like the best tequila flavored milkshake I ever tasted."

"Man milk. Nothing finer for you to drink."

I undid my bra at the back as the fastener was digging into me. I put my hand at the waistband of my skirt and looked to him for direction.

He nodded his consent at removing it. I stepped

out of my skirt, now left in only a lacy black thong and my black three-inch heels.

"Leave those on for now." He directed and then licked his lips.

I nodded.

"Now sit at the edge of the bed."

The chemistry between us was palpable. It had been since the minute we set eyes on each other in the bar. I licked my lips greedily. He was going to fuck me good I could tell. He was going to fuck me hard. I guessed I'd be leaving this room hardly able to walk and exhausted. Thank God, I had taken the rest of the day off! I would need a hot shower and my bed.

I positioned myself at the edge of the bed as he ordered. H stripped off the rest of his clothes, and Jesus was it a sight to behold! I hadn't been treated with such a display even when I had gone to see stripper shows. He removed his jacket first, folding it carefully and placing it over the back of a chair. H's every move was meticulous. His eyes fixed on mine as he unbuttoned his shirt. His hooded eyes imprisoned mine. He did it oh-so-slowly, revealing a rock-hard body with abs I could have bounced hammers off. The 'V' down to his groin made me stifle a moan.

"You like what you see?"

I nodded and licked my lips.

"Touch me. See if it feels as good as it looks."

He knelt between my legs and I ran my hands over the contours of his body. It did indeed feel like I had imagined it would. Taut. Smooth. I felt a drip of cum slide from my pussy out into the hem of my thong. I was soaking wet for him. He leaned over and blew on a nipple, making it peak even further under his ministrations. I could have hung his fucking jacket on it. Then he sucked it into his mouth, the warmth from his tongue contrasting with the cold air he blew before. I squirmed in place, desperate to have him take me, my walls already contracting with the thought of him there. He swapped to the other breast and sucked. Jesus, I could feel my pussy throb. I was so close to coming and he hadn't even touched me there yet.

He sat back, leaving me deprived. "This wasn't how my email started was it? If I recall, it started with you taking my cock in your mouth." He stood up with his dick in his hand. I swallowed. I would have to fit that in my mouth.

"Open wide, Tiff." He said, with a devilish grin that pulled at his lips.

I opened my mouth, and he pushed the tip of his cock in, pulling back out and repeating. In and out, in and out, teasing. I ran my tongue around the tip and up the underside, tasting his pre-cum again. I had to stretch my mouth wide for the girth. He pushed in a little deeper, then pulled back out, deeper again, then back out. The next time he pushed in, I sucked hard, and he groaned. He rammed his cock in as far as he could, right to the back of my throat, and I continued to suck as if my life depended on it. My jaw ached with the stretch and drool ran out the corner of my mouth. He collected it on his fingers and rubbed it into his dick. He positioned his hands behind my head and fisted one into my hair just like he said he would. "Make me come." He commanded.

I took over from his hand, holding his dick in my own hand. Wrapping my fist around the base of his shaft, I licked him from base to tip, swirling my tongue around his head. Then I took him back in my mouth. I remembered some advice I read in a magazine about doing shorter and longer sucks. H groaned and rocked himself in time with the sucks, realizing what I was doing. My jaw ached so much I was in pain, but I didn't care. It mixed with the pleasure. I looked up at H's face and his eyes were closed, his face showing he had given himself over to my mouth. Though I might be doing his bidding, right now it felt like I held all the power. I used the fingers of my spare hand to tease his balls, cupping them in my hand one at a time, stroking them and then running my fingernails down each one.

"Christ." He groaned.

H withdrew from my mouth and stroked the side of my face. "I'm not coming in your mouth today. I'm going to cum all over those gorgeous fucking tits."

He used his fist in my hair to pull me onto my feet. My legs felt unsteady. I was so goddamn horny.

"Lie back on the bed and hold your tits together, leaving me a channel for my cock."

I placed myself on the bed with my head on the pillows and did as he said. He knelt astride me and leaned over, removing the pillows from underneath my head and instead placing one under my chest so it was more pronounced than the rest of me. "Push them together now, that's right."

He pushed his dick between my large breasts and I held my boobs together as he began to move in and out. He slid in and out of the channel I had created for him a few times and then he stopped and withdrew. "Wait."

He walked over to his jacket pocket and withdrew a small bottle of massage oil and then he returned to sitting astride me. Loosening the bottle lid, he poured the oil into his hands; some of it splashed on my body giving me a hint of the cum that would shortly follow. He rubbed the oil between his hands and then rubbed it into my tits. They started to gleam as he massaged the oil in. My tits slipped out of his hands they were so greased up. "Right, where were we?" He asked.

I squished my boobs together again, and he rammed his dick between my breasts, getting faster and faster with each stroke. "One day you're going to titty fuck me from above and you will have to work for my cum in your face, but now I need to fucking finish. Clasp your hands together over the top of your tits."

I did as he ordered, and it meant my boobs were more under control for him. He thrusted between them, his pre-cum mixed with the massage oil, and it made him have a smooth journey back and forth.

His breath came in short, sharp bursts and I felt his body tighten. Then with one final massive thrust, he came in a spurt that landed partly on my neck and partly on my chin. I let go of my breasts, and he grabbed the middle of his cock, rubbing it with his hand and pushing out the last of his cum onto my chest. Then he put his fingers in it and scooping up a pile he rubbed it all over my lips. "Now that's what I was imagining. Your pretty, pink pouty lips covered in my cream. Now lick your lips."

I did as he asked. I felt hot and feverish and completely out of control. He dipped a finger, pushed my soaking wet thong aside and pushed his digit into me. I couldn't help myself. I moaned loudly, unaware of my surroundings for a moment as I lost myself in the feelings that were coursing through my pussy. I was so close to the edge and about to burst.

"Hmm, I think we'll leave it there," he said in a deep, playful voice.

My eyes widened in panic.

"Oh, if only you could see your desperate little face the way I can, baby girl. What do you want me to do to you?"

"I want you to fuck me."

"You want my ten inches stretching that tight little hole of yours?"

"Yes." I felt my pussy get wetter at the thought.

"Go stand by the window."

What?

"I- I can't do that. Someone could see us."

"That's what makes it even more exciting, kitten."

I walked over to the window. The view of the

beach was stunning, yet all I wanted to do was look at H and how his face hungered for me.

He stood behind me and I felt his cock, once again rock-hard, against my ass. He left me and dragged over the chair to the window.

"Put your left foot up on the chair."

I did, and my heel sank into the plush seat.

"I might damage the chair with my heel."

"Fuck, I hope so, or I'm doing something wrong."

I was slightly back from the window, so it was doubtful I could be seen, but the thought excited me. Who would believe the heeled realtor was on the eighth floor having her brains fucked out by her client?

Once again behind me, H put his gym-honed arms around my body and grabbed a firm hold of my breasts. "Got to make sure these babies don't escape my grip with them being all oiled up." He kneaded them with his hands, then let go to flick my nipples. Once again, his flicks connected the sensation in my nipple to a pulse between my legs. He stopped to pull my thong down and off my legs. From our reflection in the window I saw him sniff the crotch of the thong. "I'll be taking this with me to play with tonight." H threw them toward his own pile of clothing.

Grabbing his cock, already sheathed with a condom, he held it against my entrance. He slowly rubbed his thick head against my slit and I swear to God I almost came from that sensation alone.

"Are you ready for me, Tiff? I'm going to stretch you wide."

"Yes, please fuck me now. I'm so close."

With those words he thrust hard, his cock making my channel expand to fit him. Oh fuck, the feeling of fullness within me was incredible. Then he started to move. He thrust his cock in me. I rose on the balls of my feet with each thrust and then back down, my left heel sinking again into the chair cushion. He thrust even harder and faster and my walls relaxed further to accommodate him. I couldn't believe how easily my pussy had accepted his huge length. I caught sight of myself in the reflection from the window. My eyes were glazed. I was wanton with lust and looked like the star of a porn movie.

H fisted one hand around his girth and slammed into me as he brought his other hand around to the front of me and stroked my clit.

"Oh my fucking god, oh my fucking god. Yes, yes, please more."

"My name is H." He growled. "When you

demand an orgasm, you scream my name." He thrust again, his balls slamming into my ass.

"H, please, make me come." I panted, riding toward the edge.

He strummed my clit with his finger, hard and fast, matching his thrusts. It was too much for me. I couldn't take any more and started to peak. I soared and flew as I reached my conclusion and broke apart on his cock, tremors hitting me like an earthquake. His balls tightened and then a moment later he withdrew his cock and came all over my ass. I felt the warm spurts as they hit.

My breathing was ragged, and I needed to lie down. My legs gave way and H swept me up into his arms. He assessed the chair. "Look what you did." I cast my eyes down. There was a hole in the seat of the chair. Fuck. My client would go insane.

H laid me back down on the bed and then went into the bathroom. I heard him wash himself. He returned with two towels. One he had dampened, the other one dry. He wiped me down with the damp cloth and dried me with the other.

"How am I going to explain that these towels got used?"

"Do clients not usually use the bathroom?" H asked.

"No, they tend to use the facilities downstairs."

"I'll take care of it. Nothing money can't fix."

I was reminded of how I was a realtor and he was a successful businessman. I was just a plaything and would probably never see him again. I gave my thanks to fate or whatever gave me this experience that had shown me what sex could be like. Now I would never put up with an average fuck again.

We got dressed in silence. I put on my jacket and grabbed my purse.

"Could I ask you a question?" I asked quietly.

"Sure."

"Did you actually want to view the condo at all or was it all a set up to get into my panties?"

H picked up my thong and waved them in front of me. "These panties?" He asked as his lip curled into a grin, then he placed them in his pocket.

I bit my lip.

"No, I'm interested in the condo, though obviously I had imagined what might happen here. Turns out my imagination was lacking; the reality was much more pleasing."

I smiled. "I'm so glad I didn't disappoint."

"You certainly didn't, Miss Harris," he smiled, and I realized we were back to our professional business selves. "I would like to make an offer on the condo." He picked up the chair. "And you can explain that the strange gentleman making the offer took the chair he damaged with him and left a check for twenty thousand dollars in its place."

I gasped. That amount of money was obscene.

"I'm going to put this chair in my own bedroom in Manhattan and tonight when I drape my jacket across the back of it, I'll think of you grinding your heel into the seat as I ground my cock into your wet cunt."

He looked around the room.

"Well, though basic, this bedroom proved adequate for my needs. However, I'm sure I can get an interior designer to make the entire place my own."

"I'm sure you can."

"I'll be in touch, Miss Harris. Expect an email from me within the next few days."

"Okay," I nodded, and I held out my hand to shake his. "It was a pleasure to meet you, Mr. Carter."

"Oh, the pleasure was all mine. Please pay close attention to your emails. I'm very controlling about having my precise instructions followed."

"Duly noted, Mr. Carter."

"Just one thing before we leave." He turned to

me. A finger at his lip as if he was contemplating his next words. "Have you ever had two men at once?"

"What? *No, I have not.*" I snapped and turning on my heel, I walked out of the room, letting the door slam behind me, even though I was not allowed to leave a client in a property. Well, fuck it.

I heard his laughter behind me, fading as I moved further away.

CHAPTER THREE

Tiffany

I would have run to my car, except I wasn't sure if I would have remained standing due to the lack of energy after that marathon session. I had never had sex like that in my life. My feelings were so jumbled. I didn't know whether I'd had the most amazing time, or if I was just really pissed off with myself for submitting to H's seduction. Oh, who was I trying to kid? I'd had the time of my fucking life, literally. I could barely keep my eyes open, which wasn't great for my drive home. Also, my mind kept replaying what had just happened. I decided to stay behind the wheel for a moment. I closed my eyes and let my mind and body revisit the past hour or so.

Jeez, that body. He was so goddamn hard. If I had a garden, I'd like a statue of that body in it to look at every day. And his cock. Jesus Christ! I had never seen anything like that in my life.

But then he had to spoil it. Ask me if I had ever had a three-way. Two men at the same time. What fucking planet was that man on? I could hardly manage his huge cock, never mind juggle him and another guy at the same time. My traitorous core clenched at the fantasy as my thoughts ran rapidly through my mind. What did he mean? Like a taking turns kind of scenario, or one in my pussy and one in my ass? I felt myself grow wet again which wasn't great considering he kept my panties as some kind of trophy and my juices were going to run straight down my leg and onto my skirt. No more daydreaming, Tiff, I told myself. Well, at least until I got home.

The apartment was empty being that my two girl friends were busy showing properties. Thank god I wasn't competing with Kayla for our bathroom. I headed to my room and stripped off all my clothes. As I looked down, I realized that H had sucked a love-bite onto the side of my breast. I ran over it with my fingers. I carried fresh towels into the bathroom and decided to soak in the tub and began to run the bath. Before steam misted up the mirror, I turned and gazed at my reflection in it. Did I look any different? I felt more confident as a lover, like I actually knew more of what sex could be about. Totally losing myself in the moment. Complete abandon. I stroked between my legs with my fingers. I was sore from being stretched by that ten-inch monster. As I lowered myself into the tub, it stung slightly between my legs, but the heat from the bathwater worked on my muscles and soothed away any tension I had brought home with me. I placed my head back on my bath pillow and once again lost myself in thoughts of what had just happened. I stayed there until the water cooled and then dragged myself out of the tub. Wrapping my body in a huge towel and my hair in a small one, I returned to my room, where I quickly dried my hair and changed into some pajamas. I couldn't crawl under my duvet fast enough; my eyes were closing as I did it, and within minutes I was lost, sleeping away the exhaustion of a delightful fuck.

When I woke and checked my alarm clock it was five in the afternoon. Shit! I had slept for hours. Under my duvet was cozy and warm and I didn't feel like getting out, but I knew I should, or I would never sleep tonight. Sighing, I swung myself out of bed and after a quick bathroom trip, I wrapped a robe around myself and headed into the kitchen for a coffee. I couldn't be bothered to get dressed again. I had no plans for the night, so I would leave my pjs on. I wondered if anyone else picked their night outfit according to their mood? Often, I slept in shorts and a t-shirt, but sometimes comfy pjs were required. Especially when you had been given the orgasm of your life and it had wiped you out. I rubbed my jaw; it was ever so slightly achy. Unsurprising given the workout it had performed. I fired up my laptop at the table and checked my messages but there were no pervy messages from H. There were however business emails pertaining to the sale of the apartment and a celebratory email from my boss congratulating me on a job well done. Apparently, H had informed him that I was a consummate professional and a member of staff to be proud of. Huh? So maybe he didn't mean it when he said he would be in touch in that way? Perhaps I misinterpreted what he had said to me. Could I have misheard his two men comment? I couldn't help feeling disappointed about the fact he might not want a repeat performance. But I did know one thing. I would never chase a man. Been there done that and it had blown up in my face. One of my exes had stopped messaging me and I had discovered it was because his wife had taken his phone from him. Never again. If it was meant to be, he would get in touch with me. I slammed my laptop shut, annoyed with myself. Why was I making such a big deal out of a not-so-quick fuck? I'd had a good time. Hell, I'd had a great time. End of story. One for the memory banks on a hot evening flying solo.

I went over to the kitchen area and started prepping spaghetti for us all for our evening meal.

The girls came in just after seven and arrived within ten minutes of each other. Shoes and jackets were discarded around the room with sighs of relief that feet were no longer in heels. I handed them each a glass of wine and told them dinner would be ready in ten.

"You got home early?" Kayla asked.

"I got home hours ago. I made the sale and rewarded myself with the rest of the day off."

"So, what did you do all day? The apartment doesn't look any tidier." She joked.

"I slept. Today was exhausting."

"You might want to check in with your physician because if showing houses is making you so tired..." added Haley, "sounds like you might need a vitamin or two."

Kayla shook her head. "No, Haley. There's something she's not telling us. Look at her face. She has a little uplift at the corner of her mouth and she's flushed in the face. She only gets that when she has no idea whether to blurt out gossip or not. Spill, bitch."

"Oh look. Dinner's ready." I told them, trying not to laugh.

"Only a small portion for me. I'm meeting Malcolm tonight and don't expect me back," Haley said smiling.

"Malcolm from Green's? When did that happen?" I asked as I filled my plate.

"He asked me out on a date last week, but I needed to think about it. I wasn't totally sure about dating someone from the company. Anyway, today he brought me flowers, so I said I would meet him tonight for a drink."

Kayla and I met each other's gaze. Haley looked at both of us.

"It's not like that. He's really nice. Although I hope he's not too nice." She said with a devilish grin.

"Haley!" I said. "Are you hoping for a booty call tonight?"

She sighed. "It's been a while. It would be nice."

We took our seats around the table, and I finished off and refilled my glass of wine because I could see Kayla staring at me and knew it was only a matter of time before her twenty-questions started.

"So, how did the condo showing go? Did the client go for it?"

I nodded. "He did. He was very impressed with the place."

"So, who was he? Anyone we know?"

"His name is Henry Carter."

Kayla's eyes lit up. "Oh, he's hot. I've seen his photos in the papers. Totally loaded in the pants and in the wallet from what I have heard."

I blushed. She caught it.

"Oh my god, what are you not telling us? Spill!"

I took another gulp of my wine. "You know that disgusting email I read out to you?"

"The one with all the filthy things that man wanted to do to you, or you to him? Yes?"

"Well..."

"No!" Kayla's eyes widened. "It was him?"

I nodded. "Yup, Henry Carter is H."

"Holy shit! So, what happened? Did he come on to you? Lean in and kiss you? How did it play out?"

"She might not want to tell you, Kayla. She might want to keep it private, you know?" Haley said. "Though I hope not because we want all the juicy details." She pulled her chair closer to mine. Kayla laughed and did the same with her chair.

I sighed. Then I told them everything that happened from the moment I had met him in the bar to the moment I had left to get in my car.

"Holy fucking Christ. I think I'm going to have to go get my vibrator just from your verbal replay." Kayla said and then let out a laugh.

"I really hope I'm getting fucked tonight." Haley frowned.

"Ten inches? Ten fucking inches and wide too? Does he have a brother? Scratch that," Kayla smirked and then grabbed her laptop. "I'll check for myself."

"Kayla, eat the damn dinner I made for us. Haley's out tonight. We'll curl up on the sofa with the rest of the bottle of wine and do a full internet search."

"You're on."

"DO I LOOK ALL RIGHT?" Haley asked. I wished she was a bit more confident. She was so pretty, but always hid herself in tent-like dresses because she was embarrassed about her big ass. She was wearing a red dress that reached her knees and she did look nice. It suited her petite frame.

I checked out the back of it. "Easily unzipped and off. Yes, it passes."

She smiled. "That's why I chose it."

It was good to see her getting herself back on the dating scene. It had been a while and I think her confidence took a hit from her last boyfriend who had told her she was hopeless in bed because she refused to give him a blow job one night. Apparently, he wasn't all that great on the hygiene. Made me feel sick thinking about it.

"I'll lock the door behind you. Grab your purse," I told her.

As I opened the door, I saw a guy walk out of the apartment opposite ours. It had been vacant up until last week and this was the first time we had seen any hint of a new tenant. He stopped and stared at us.

And I'm very sure both of us stared back at him, because he was around six foot four, with short dark brown hair, shaved at the sides and longer on top. He had a very of-the-moment beard and mustache. He was wearing tight-fitting jeans, and a navy t-shirt that showed a sleeve of tattoos on his corded left arm. More tattoos poked out from around his neckline.

"Hey, neighbors. I was gonna come and introduce myself tomorrow, but I guess there's no time like the present. Unless you're in a rush?" He nodded toward Haley. It was at that point I realized I was standing there in my pjs and robe. Jesus, what a first impression.

"The elevator can wait a few minutes. Hey there, I'm Haley. Haley Martin." Haley held out her hand very formally, and he shook it.

"I'm Brandon. Brandon Bailey." They dropped hands and he turned to me and held his arm outstretched for a handshake.

I noted his long fingers. My mom used to call them piano fingers. I compared them to the meaty digits that were in me earlier. He stared at me. Christ, was he reading my mind? Then I realized I had left him holding his arm out while I daydreamed.

I shook his hand. "I'm Tiffany Harris, seeing that we're doing the formal thing with the handshakes and surnames and all."

He laughed, exposing a row of perfect white teeth. Fuck me, was he an actor or something?

"No, I'm not an actor." He smiled as the amusement washed over his face.

What the fuck? Had I said it out loud?

"Nothing as exciting as that. I'm a fitness instructor."

Haley received a text on her cell. "I have to run guys. My date has arrived."

"Good luck." I told her. "Hopefully we won't see you later."

"Fingers crossed," she yelled back.

"Right," I said to Brandon. Mr. Fitness Instructor.

Boy, I'd bet he could go for hours.

I chastise myself. Since earlier today I had been like some desperate horny housewife. "Well, I have to go. Things to do and all that."

"Yes, I was on my way to work."

I looked back at his jeans and t-shirt.

"Oh, I don't wear my gear there."

"I'm sorry. I'm being very rude. Ignore me, I've had a hard day. I'll be okay tomorrow after a good night's sleep."

"What do you do?" He asked.

"I'm a realtor for Green's."

"Bet you meet some interesting people in that line of work. I know I do in mine. We should share stories sometime over a coffee. A get-to-know-the-neighbor welcome coffee," he corrected, as my eyes widened and I stepped back.

"Tiff, what the fuck are you doing out there?" Kayla yelled from the room. I heard her footsteps pad closer to the door.

"Oh hey," she said to Brandon.

"This is the last roommate for you to meet." I said. "Kayla Jackson, meet Brandon Bailey."

"Fuck me, you're hot." She told him.

"Erm, thanks?" He chuckled.

"Kayla!" I scolded her.

"God, calm down. I'm just calling it like I see it. He's not my type. Sorry," she apologized. "I either like 'em young or a bit older. Come back and see if I'm single in about fifteen years, okay?"

I shook my head at her and mouthed 'I'm sorry' at Brandon.

"I found some interesting stuff on the internet search," she told me. "Don't be long."

"I am so sorry." I told Brandon. My face was flushed with the heat of my embarrassment. "I cannot believe what she just said to you. She gets worse."

"I hear worse at work, seriously. It's even more uncomfortable when they are interested. I have no problem with someone who isn't."

"Well, as a politer member of the household, a coffee would be very nice sometime. We can either have it here or we can come to you."

"Oh, don't bring the others." He said. "One's too shy and one's too bold. You. You're just right."

He winked and walked off down the corridor

toward the elevator and once again I ended up standing wide-eyed and speechless at the words from a man's mouth. Twice in one day. What were the odds?

I turned around and closing the door behind me with my foot, I clasped my robe over my chest and headed to the living room to find out what Kayla had discovered and got ready to drink a shit load of wine.

CHAPTER FOUR

Tiffany

I was daydreaming about my day's adventures while Kayla related boring pieces of information to me that she had read on the internet. He's rich. Blah. She couldn't find out anything about his private life, but he never showed up at business events with a woman on his arms.

"If he hadn't fucked you senseless, I would think he was fucking gay."

"Close the laptop now, I'm bored. Let's watch a movie."

"Oh, hang on, what's this? His name's on a

forum. Listen to this. "Henry Carter is the owner of a private members' club in New York called S. Members are not allowed to divulge what the club is about which makes it seem a little bit forbidden and naughty. If anyone can shed light on this, please let us know."

"And does anyone?" I asked.

"No." Kayla sighed.

"Well, there you go. More pointless hearsay."

"I want to go there."

"Well, you can't, can you? Because it's a private members' club which you're not invited to."

"I bet you could get us invited."

I turned to her. "Oh yeah? How do you work that out?"

"Call him. You have his number through work."

"I am not calling that man after what I did with him today. That would look needy."

"Tiff, you've been in bed all afternoon, so you aren't going to be in a rush to get to sleep. I'm bored of sitting and watching movies. Call him."

"No!" I told her. "Now I'm going to the bath-room. Go grab us some snacks and pick a movie."

I left the room. Sometimes Kayla could be a little too much. I hadn't processed what had happened today yet. I hoped to God Henry didn't report me to my employers. I started to feel nauseous. No, he wouldn't? I had received the praising email from my boss. He loved every minute of it and was the instigator after all.

I walked back in to see Kayla shutting my laptop, with a guilty expression plastered on her face.

"What have you done?" I snapped.

"Promise you won't get mad?"

"I'm already mad." I took my laptop out of her hands, opened it back up and tried to see what she had been doing. "Tell me now." I gave her my best narrowed eyed look that meant business.

"I only sent a little email."

Clicking through to my sent folder, I found Kayla had messaged Henry in response to his anonymous email of before.

I read it.

I WANT **to see the club.**

I'm intrigued.

I BREATHED A SIGH OF RELIEF. "Oh, thank fuck that's all you sent. I can live with that. I thought you were going to tell him I wanted his cock in my mouth or something."

"Well, I might have done that with a little more time, but you came back in the room too fast so I just hit send."

I shook my head. "Movie." I demanded.

She rolled her eyes and got up to choose one.

We had been watching *Deadpool* for twenty-seven minutes when there was a knock at the front door. Kayla pressed the pause button, and I dragged myself from the couch. I opened the door to find H's driver. He passed me a small square box. It was silver with a black ribbon.

"Mr. Carter asked that I wait outside for you for the next thirty minutes after you opened the box. I will leave it with you." He walked away and headed down the steps.

I closed the door and walked back into the living room, taking a seat back on the couch.

"What is it?" Kayla asked.

"It's from H."

I untied the ribbon and removed the box lid. Inside, the box was padded with black satin and on it laid a silver key with a black S on it. There was a card.

• • •

CAN'T HAVE you left wanting.

Come, see for yourself.

Matthew will drive you. Dress to impress.

KAYLA READ the message over my shoulder and squealed. "Yes! Sorry Ryan Reynolds, you're hot and all but we're going clubbing."

She dragged me off the couch. "Come on, we need to get ready."

I let her drag me toward my room. I couldn't help but be intrigued now too. I had heard of private members clubs before. Places only celebrities and the filthy rich attended. I wondered if this was one of them? They had to have somewhere to go where they wouldn't be annoyed by normal people, didn't they? Kayla was right. I wasn't the slightest bit tired. Though I irritated with her for what she had done, it was a night out. I looked through my closet. Dress to impress, right? I changed into a plain black silky bra that left no trace of lines and wriggled into a short glittery silver dress. I left panties out of the equation as they would cause a visible line in the dress. The dress had cap sleeves and a V-neck that showed a small amount of my large boobs. The tightness of the dress helped to hold my ample assets in place though it did nothing to hide them. I had bought the dress in a moment of madness, egged on by Kayla to stop hiding what I had. Tonight it was screaming at me to be worn. I wrapped a black pashmina around my shoulders just in case I found it too uncomfortable being under the gaze of others. I finished with black ankle boots that laced up my calves slightly. They had a four-inch heel.

I fixed my hair so that it was half up in a messy bun with the rest of it hanging around my face. Usually I would wear darker makeup in the evening and I stuck to a darker eye shadow, but kept the same pink lipgloss that H had smeared. I realized he wasn't forced to be there, but despite the sentence he left me with, I couldn't help but hope I saw him again tonight. I picked up my purse and headed back to the living room to wait for Kayla.

A few minutes later she joined me. Her red hair was curled in ringlets and she wore a green shift dress, with fishnet tights and black five-inch heels, which made her just a fraction taller than me.

"Ready? Let's go and have some fun." She winked.

I locked the door behind us.

. . .

AS WE WALKED down the stairs to head toward Matthew's limo, Brandon got out of a Hyundai Elantra. He whistled. "Ladies, you look mighty fine." He came around and bowed in front of us. "Where are you off to?"

"We're going to a VIP Members Club. Ssh. It's top secret. We'll explode if we give you any details. Don't wait up." Kayla winked and carried on walking to the limo.

"Well, have a nice evening." Brandon said.

"Thank you. I have no idea what to expect, but as long as there's music and alcohol, we should be fine." I smiled.

"Well, if it's not up to your standards, I have wine in my apartment." He said, smiling playfully. "Gorgeous women always welcome."

I laughed. "What a charmer. I'll see you around."

"You sure will."

I walked to the limo and nodded to Matthew and thanked him for waiting. I let him open the door to let me inside.

It took approximately twenty minutes to drive into Manhattan. Matthew turned onto East 57th Street and pulled up outside what looked like a residential building. There was some expensive real estate around here, with the skyscraper at 252 in high demand. The area was named 'Billionaires row' for a reason. Matthew handed the keys to an approaching valet and opened our doors. "Please, follow me."

He escorted us through double doors, opened by doormen dressed in smart gray suits. A very glamorous looking willowy brunette in a loose, royal-blue shift dress approached us.

Matthew spoke to her, "Could we have another silver key please, Ashley, and two chains?"

"Of course."

She went into a locked drawer underneath her desk and lifted out a key identical to the one I had. She threaded it onto a chain and then seeing the key in my hand, she passed it to Kayla.

Kayla got the idea and fixed it around her neck.

"May I?" Ashley took my key and repeated her actions. I placed the chain around my neck. The key fitted within the swell of my breasts, feeling cold against the heat from my body.

"I will leave you here," Matthew said. "When you are ready to leave, please let Ashley know you need transportation and she will take care of it."

"That's okay, we'll call a cab." I told him.

He shook his head. "Mr. Carter would want to make sure you were home safely. Please let Ashley phone one of our drivers to take you home."

"Okay." I agreed.

"Please go up in the elevator to the twenty-fourth floor. You will need to hold a key against the pad in the elevator." Ashley replied.

We thanked her and moved toward it.

The elevator doors opened. The space was large and had a black satin covered ceiling dotted with silver stars, like a beautiful night sky. I pressed the button for the twenty-fourth floor.

"I'm so excited I could piss my pants." Kayla squealed in delight.

I wished I felt the same. Instead I felt a sense of trepidation; like everyone here would be from money and we were going to look like fish out of water.

We walked across the lobby. The floor had the same pattern, black with silver stars, and doormen greeted us in front of two huge silver double doors. We had to remove our chains, so they could hold the keys up to a screen.

"First time?" One of the doormen asked. I assumed it showed up on his screen.

"Yes."

"Enjoy, and don't leave before midnight." I swore I saw a hint of a smirk at the edge of his mouth.

As we walked through the doors we gasped. The splendor of the place was incredible. There were bars at each edge of the room. A large dance floor was in the center of the room and there was a stage at one end where bands must play. Each black gloss table had a silver star in the center of it. The place was buzzing. Bottles of expensive champagne and wine were everywhere. All the men were in black tie and all the women dressed in the latest hot designers. I felt shabby in my silver dress. It looked good enough, but these women would know I wasn't dressed in designer clothes.

We headed to the bar where we both asked for a glass of white wine.

The barman—who Kayla was already flirting with—tilted his head at us. "First time here?"

"Yes," I stated, quite abruptly. "Is it really that obvious?"

He smiled, "Yes, because you asked for white wine when you have a silver key. No one likes asking for champagne on their first visit."

"I can't afford champagne." I told him. "I don't know if I'll be able to afford the wine yet."

Now the bartender's face was marred with

confusion. "You have a silver key membership. All drinks are included."

"Whoop," Kayla hollered. "In that case we'll have a bottle of Moet and two glasses, darling."

"Kayla!"

"What?" She gave a faux look of guilt. "We're here to enjoy ourselves. By the way, have you seen stud muffin yet?"

"No." I had looked for H ever since we walked in to the building, but he didn't seem to be here. I couldn't help feeling a little disappointed, but it was time to drink, dance, and enjoy ourselves as this membership was probably a one-time only thing and we needed a night to remember.

A SIREN WENT off at ten minutes to midnight, making us jump. The other members wore faces filled with emotions like trepidation and excitement. They passed knowing smiles and looks amongst each other. Kayla and I were totally confused. The atmosphere in the place had changed. Something was about to happen, and I guessed that the siren was the precursor.

An older gentleman with salt and pepper hair climbed the stairs to the stage and switched on the microphone. People moved closer to him, standing on the dance floor.

"What's happening?" Kayla asked.

I shrugged, not knowing myself. "Maybe there's a band coming on?"

The man spoke into the microphone. "Good evening, ladies and gentlemen. It's now time for the auction. Please welcome onto the stage William and Jesse."

"Auction?" I whispered at Kayla. "Goddamn rich people. Bet they're selling paintings or jewelry."

But when William and Jesse walked onto the stage, I realized I couldn't have been more wrong...

CHAPTER FIVE

Tiffany

They were naked. Completely and utterly stark naked. Kayla almost choked on her drink. William was short and muscular with sleeves of tattoos and a buzz cut. His dick was soft. It looked average sized but quite thick. Jesse was tall and leaner though still ripped. His cock stood erect at about eight inches and appeared to have a small bend to it. They stood either side of the suited gentleman who didn't blink at the fact he was flanked by two naked men.

"Please gather your paddles. The auction is about to commence."

I realized that some people had paddles in their hands. They were silver stars on a stick with numbers across the star.

"What the hell is going on?" I asked Kayla.

"Fucked if I know. How do I get one of those paddle things? I want to bid if I get to win a date with one of those hunks."

We watched spellbound as people bid on the men until finally a woman won the auction with a bid of twenty thousand dollars.

"Thank you." The man said into the microphone. "The rooms will now open, and the main act will be on stage at one am."

"Well, well, well," Kayla said with a smirk on her face. "If I'm not mistaken, I'm guessing your Mr. Carter owns a sex club."

The lights came up and doormen opened several doors around the main room. The doors had looked like the rest of the paneling on the walls, which is why we hadn't noticed them before. People started to disappear through the doors.

"Oh my god." I said.

Kayla laughed. "I was so not expecting this. Shall we go look?"

"No." I clutched her arm. "What if they want us to join in? We don't know the rules here."

She sighed. "Yeah, you're right. Let's get another bottle of champagne and get ready for the main act at one."

A CURTAIN HAD BEEN DRAWN across the stage. At ten to one, the siren had gone off again and quite a few members made their way back from the rooms into the main bar area. It didn't take a genius to figure out that the messed-up hair, reddened faces and disheveled clothes meant that they had more than likely just fucked, or at least played around. At one am, some soft music began to play, and the curtain drew back to reveal a bed.

The woman who had won the auction, a slim woman who looked in her mid-forties, was lying on the bed. She was—like the men before her—completely naked. Her pert breasts were small, and she was displaying a completely shaved pussy. She was propped up on a pillow and pretending to read a book.

The music stopped, and William and Jesse walked onto the stage.

William took the book from the woman's hand and placed it on the floor. Then he took the hand that had clutched the book and placed it on his cock.

She stroked it until it grew. Jesse had been sitting at the end of the bed. He walked over, stood beside William, and getting the woman to sit up and perch on the side of the bed, he took her other hand and placed it on his cock.

I couldn't believe my eyes.

And for once in her life, I think Kayla was speechless too.

The woman pumped both cocks at the same time, looking to the guys for direction. They got her to lie back on the bed with her legs slightly apart. William sat at her head and made her take his cock in her mouth while Jesse held her ankles and plunged his mouth onto her clit. I watched as the woman bucked up off the bed in pleasure. As the cock left her mouth, loud moans began to escape from her. After coming through tongue-fucking, she was positioned on her knees on the bed. Jesse got behind her and unravelling a condom onto his cock, he held her by the hips and pushed his hard cock into her pussy. She screamed with pleasure. At the front of her, William sucked on one breast, then another, while his fingers played with her clit. The woman's head was back, lips apart, and she was moaning and wailing like a teenage girl seeing their rock idol in real life.

"This is so fucking hot." Kayla said, licking her lips.

To be honest, I had been so engrossed, I had forgotten she was there.

Both guys took turns fucking her and the performance ended with her swallowing Jesse's cum while William sprayed his across her tits.

The curtains closed, and the audience broke out in an ecstatic applause.

Coming back to my surroundings, I realized that I was soaking wet. Soaking wet and wearing no panties. I excused myself to go to the bathroom.

"There'll be more than you in there playing with yourself." Kayla said laughing.

"I'm not going to do that. Jesus, girl. I need a pee." I told her.

She took a sip of her champagne and winked at me.

As I made my way over to the bathroom, my phone vibrated in my purse. I picked it up, but waited until I had the light from the bathroom to help me read the message.

Mr. Carter: So, is the thought of two men still offensive to you?

Oh my God! He must be here!

I texted him back.

Tiffany: I guess that's for me to know and you to find out. But it's way past my bedtime now, and I'm leaving. Thank you for my key.

A moment later another beep indicated another text message.

Mr. Carter: Well you gave me a brand-new key today; it seemed only fair to return the favor. By the way, that's a life-time membership at the highest level for you and your friend. Let me know if Haley wishes to join.

Jesus. He knew the names of my friends. What else did he know about me?

I sat on the bathroom seat and changed his name on my phone over to H. It fit better. After today's events, I didn't think the formality of Mr. Carter suited anymore.

Leaving the bathroom, I grabbed Kayla, and we called it a night, accepting H's transport to take us home.

. . .

I GOT IN BED, but I couldn't sleep. Thoughts of the day and the night whirled around my mind. When H had mentioned two men, I had been appalled, and yet watching that woman tonight on the stage, I couldn't deny that I had been completely turned on. I pictured how one had fucked her pussy while another fucked her mouth. I assumed she wasn't into anal as they hadn't fucked her ass and pussy together. Between my legs, I started to feel wet with my daydreaming (or should that be nightdreaming?) and I grabbed one of my breasts as I remembered how one of the guys had took her breast in his mouth. In my imagination the scene changed to me lying on that bed and the man sucking on my breasts became H. Where the woman's breasts had been small and pert, H grabbed mine roughly, pushing and pulling on them and biting on my nipples. I pinched my nipples as I imagined his bite, remembering that one of my breasts had a love-bite on it from earlier that day.

Dream H moved his fingers down my body and trailed his middle finger to plunge in my wet pussy. I drenched his finger with my juices and moaned. Coming back to myself, I blushed as I realized I was in my room. I figured Kayla would be fast asleep by now, and Haley was already asleep in her room when we got back as we'd heard her soft snores, but I didn't want anyone hearing my moans and masturbation. I closed my eyes, mindful to keep as quiet as I could, and I plunged my fingers back into myself pretending it was H. But my fingers just weren't enough for this fantasy, and I found myself wanting, on the brink. I switched on my bedside light and opened one of the drawers in my nightstand I took out my dildo. It was purple and a close match to a real penis although harder in texture. It was seven inches so nowhere near H's massive cock, but it would do. I made a mental note to go to a sex store and buy a larger one. He had spoiled me with his large cock—average sized vibrators and dildos were not going to cut it now!

I turned off the light and got back under my duvet. With the dildo in my hand, I let my mind take me back to where I had left my fantasy. Now H was asking me to take his cock in my mouth. I shoved the dildo between my lips and tongued it, pretending he was begging me to fuck it. To get my fantasy to play out as the woman's scene had however, I needed another man. I had not found Jesse or William very attractive, so I didn't want them in my visual. I tried to imagine a mystery man, but my thoughts wouldn't play ball. Then he snuck in—Brandon. I felt my cheeks flush as thoughts of him joining us came into my mind and wouldn't leave. In my mind, Brandon had appeared from the edge of the room. He stalked over to me. He was dressed in a t-shirt and board shorts. His huge dick tented his shorts. He came closer and demanded that I pull them down. As I did, his cock sprang next to my face. He looked at H and communicating with their eyes, H removed his cock from my mouth and Brandon thrust his in.

"Suck me hard, bitch."

In reality, in my room, I felt my cum run down my leg, I was so turned on.

H moved himself between my legs and growled, "I'm going to fuck your pussy, while Brandon fucks your mouth, and you will love it."

I removed the dildo from my mouth and positioned it at my entrance. Oh, how I wished I had two dildos! I pistoned three fingers of my left hand and stuck them in my mouth while I held my dildo at the entrance of my pussy. Then I shoved the dildo hard inside myself, thrusting it in and out. It was hard to coordinate, but I tried to thrust my fingers in my mouth at the same time, imagining that both Brandon and H were fucking each hole at once. I came hard and I couldn't help but let out a cry as my body bucked. My orgasm had shaken my body, the force of it so intense. I had never come like that alone before. What had H unleashed in me? I laid back, the dildo abandoned at the side of me. Aftershocks shook my body and my heart thudded in my chest. I felt dizzy; that's how hard my orgasm had taken me. When I calmed down, I put my fingers to my pussy. I was soaked and used my shorts to mop between my legs. Then another thought came to me. I gathered some of the wetness from between my legs and smeared it over and in my asshole. Then I grabbed the dildo and nudged it at my entrance. I was an anal sex virgin and other than a past boyfriend sticking a digit in it once or twice, nothing had breached my puckered hole. Relaxing, I nudged the dildo, letting it push in a little, but it was no good. Though I was intrigued, my ass wasn't playing along. It stayed tight and unyielding. I could feel my eyes start to close, so I gave up and let sleep overtake my body. My alarm was set for six-thirty am and it was four am now. I was sure going to need that coffee in a couple hours, but with a last sigh, I decided it had been totally worth it.

CHAPTER SIX

Tiffany

I dragged myself into the living room at twenty-to-seven after allowing myself one snooze of the alarm clock. I knew that if I hadn't got out of bed at that point, I would have never gotten up that morning.

Haley snorted when she saw me, then she nodded her head toward Kayla, who was laid on the couch. "What on earth were you two doing that has you so dead this morning?"

"We went to a club, a sex club." Kayla blurted out, mumbling through the cushion her face was resting on.

"What?!" Haley gasped. Her face paled, and her eyes widened.

I sat at the table with my freshly poured coffee. "We looked up H on the net, and Kayla found out he owned a club. Long story short, we went. It seemed like a normal, but posh nightclub. Then at midnight it all changed. Rooms were opened, and there was an auction held to perform on the stage. A woman had a ménage with two guys in front of us all."

Haley's jaw drops. "For real?"

"Yep, and H gave us a free membership that included drinks, so we consumed far too much champagne and were so stunned and intrigued that we stayed to watch. Then we had even more alcohol while we tried to digest what we had just seen."

"Seriously, it was hot." Kayla mumbled. "We didn't see what happened in any of the side rooms, but you could take a wild guess looking at the people who left them."

"Oh, by the way, H texted me and said that you could have a membership if you wanted one too. Somehow he knows exactly who I live with."

"He texted you? When?" Kayla sat up on the couch looking more animated.

"Yes, just the once last night. Oh, and our memberships are lifetime. He asked me what I thought about the ménage. I think he's hoping I'll have a three-way with him."

"Would you?" Haley asked, then blushed. She really could be innocent sometimes. "I can't even get one lover, never mind two at once."

"Oh god, I forgot. How was your date with Malcolm last night? How did it go?" I asked.

"It didn't go. That was the problem. We had drinks and then we went back to his place. He couldn't get it up, and he blamed me. Said it had never happened to him before. Maybe it is me? He's not the first to suggest I'm hopeless in bed, is he? I think I need lessons. Maybe I'll go to that club and let people use me for practice."

Me and Kayla laughed at the same time. I was imagining Haley on the bed on stage saying 'just come fuck me'. As if! Kayla basically said what I was thinking.

"Haley, there is no way you would get on that stage. You would die of embarrassment."

"Well, maybe that's the whole point." She retorted with her hands on her hips. "I'm getting nowhere being this version of Haley. I might need to reinvent myself."

I got up from my seat and walked over to hug her. "Listen to me. You're perfect just the way you are. Don't even try to change yourself for other people. The guys you have been out with are straight up assholes. That's what you need to change. Choose a different kind of man."

She sighed. "Well now I have to face Malcolm today."

"If he gives you any grief, wave your pinkie finger at him and make it droop down. He'll shut his mouth real quick. No guy wants news of his lack of keeping an erection circulating round the staff and that's what he'll get if he's not careful." Kayla told her.

Haley smiled at Kayla. "Thanks for having my back."

"Anyway, back to you." Kayla's eyes were on me. "So, would you be up for a three-way with H?"

I squirmed on my seat. "Well, yesterday morning I was completely offended by the suggestion. But after last night, I'm not so sure. That woman seemed to be really enjoying herself. I have to admit I'm a little more open to the idea now."

"Well, you would certainly need to be open. Your mouth and your thighs." Kayla shot back with a wink. Then she burst out laughing.

"I guess like most women, I have been trying to get a guy who I could settle down with. The whole white picket fence and kids thing. Maybe before I look for that kind of a commitment, I should allow myself the opportunity to experiment if it comes my way."

"Won't be the only thing coming your way."

I groaned at her. "Please, stop. I haven't had enough sleep to put up with your humor."

"Go get ready, you two, and I'll make us more coffee to take in with us. I hope your schedules aren't too full today because I have a feeling you aren't going to be your usual sparkling selves. Go on, shoo. Tiff, you can use my bathroom to save time."

"Thank you, sweetheart. I'll be quick, and I'll leave it as I found it." I kissed her cheek and headed for the shower, hoping that a few minutes under the cold water would wake me up, although if the strong coffee hadn't worked it was seriously doubtful.

In the shower I once again noted the love-bite on my breast. I ran my fingers down it. I couldn't believe it had only happened yesterday. I thought about my schedule for today. It was going to be so boring in comparison! While I had drunk my coffee, I had checked my messages on the laptop but there was nothing from H. Maybe he would never contact me again, and I had just been a conquest? Maybe he only wanted me to contact him again if I was open to the idea of two men? I pushed the thought to the back of my mind. I needed to get out of the shower and get to work. Properties needed to be sold. As I thought of the word SOLD, I was back to the woman at the auction. To feel comfortable enough to bid for a slice of sexy action on a public stage? I couldn't imagine it, and with that, I blasted the shower onto cold to get my mind off sex and onto the day ahead.

THE REST of the week passed by quickly, with us all immersed in our work. I had to go in on Saturday too as I had so much work to do, but hey, it paid my bills. Sunday, I laid in bed until lunchtime and then spent the rest of the day just chilling around the apartment. On Sunday evening, there was a knock on the door. Kayla and Haley have gone to the movies, so I put my robe on and answered it. It was Brandon. Fuck me, I was in my robe again.

"I do get dressed, honestly." I laughed.

"I know, I saw you all dressed up the other night, remember?"

"Ah, that you did!"

"Well, I was checking in because despite my offering you coffee, you haven't taken me up on it. I sat in my apartment thinking I could either get really down about it and feel rejected, or I could come ask you again. So, would you like a coffee sometime?"

"I can do one better, Haley and Kayla are out. If you don't mind me being in my robe and pjs, I have wine that I'm willing to share?"

"Perfect." He smiled.

I stood back and let him in.

"Just kick your shoes off anywhere and excuse the mess. We work hard, play hard, but don't clean hard I'm afraid."

I watched Brandon look around the apartment. Thank goodness it was littered with magazines and nail polishes and not our underwear.

"I have two sisters. It reminds me of home."

I got the bottle of wine and two glasses and we got to know each other, chatting about our backgrounds and families. He was easy to talk to, and by the time a couple of hours had passed, I felt like I had known him for years. Of course, he was also easy on the eyes and as the wine had gone down, he had gotten sexier and sexier. I kept thinking of my fantasy from earlier in the week and blushed.

"Look at you, wine makes your face flush. You're all pink." Brandon leaned over and touched my cheek. "Your cheeks are burning!"

Of course, I blushed even more then.

"Stop tormenting me. You're making it worse."

"Hmmm, is it the wine, or are you enjoying my hot gym body? Is that it?"

I must have been almost a dark shade of red by now and I hid my face in my hands.

He grabbed my hands and moved them away. "Hey, I'm sorry. I was having a little fun. I don't handle wine well obviously, I'm used to beer. I hope I didn't offend you?"

"No, not at all." I laughed.

"What's funny?"

"Well, now I want to know if you do have a hot gym body, or if under those clothes you look like Mr. Bean."

He dropped his jaw in mock offence. "How dare you question my gym bod. Do you know how many women would love to spend the evening with it?"

"Sorry, I think you're going to have to show me."

What the fuck have I just said? What is wrong with me? I've become a fucking slut.

He lifted his sweater and tee and pulled them off over his head. I gasped in shock as tanned, taut skin was revealed. He had an eight pack. From his neck down over his pec at the left-hand side was a tattoo of a steampunk-style clock. His arms were threaded muscle, and he looked like he could lift me with just one of them. I stared down the sleeve of tattoos on his left arm: skulls, stars with writing in them, a series of interlocking gears. He was lean, but oh so solid. I reached over and ran my hands down his chest. He watched as I trailed my palms down him, all the way down to his lower abdomen and then back up.

He swallowed audibly. Then he caught my hand.

"Sorry." I shook my head. "It's the wine. I'm not usually like this. God, I'm so sorry. I don't want you to think the wrong thing."

"I think I'm in an apartment with a sexy as fuck woman and she just asked me to strip and touched my chest. I'm wondering whether to go and splash my face with cold water because I've got to be dreaming. Can I try something?" He asked.

I nodded. "Sure."

He sat on the couch at the side of me and leaned in. His mouth crashed on mine. Warmth seeped through my lips, and my mouth opened to accept his tongue. I tasted the wine on him. I kissed him back hard, and we launched into a frenzy of movement. My hands stroked his chest again. His hand slipped inside my robe and under my top, grasping one of my breasts.

"Jesus, your tits. Let me see them."

I opened my robe and pulled up my top, exposing my magnificent orbs in all their glory.

He pushed his head in between them and holding them at either side made groaning noises.

"Fuck, I'm going to come in my boxers from this alone."

He took a nipple in his mouth and sucked hard. Thank goodness, the love-bite from Monday had gone. I opened the button of his pants and lowered the zipper. He lifted himself to help me. I freed his cock and licked my lips. It had to be at least the same size as H's. It was huge! It was a little less wide than H's but was no less impressive.

"Fuck, you're huge."

"Eleven inches." He replied.

Eleven! My face must have looked worried. I'd had a hard time handling ten.

"Don't worry. I know what I'm doing with it and we'll manage."

He guided my hand to his cock, and I started to stroke him.

A loud laugh came from outside and I sprang back away from him.

"Oh God, the girls are back."

"Fuck!" Brandon grunted. He quickly pulled up

his pants, zipped them, and shucked on his t-shirt and sweater.

The only thing I had to do was let my top fall back down and pull my robe tighter. God, I was fucking horny. So horny I had lost track of time.

The girls let themselves into the apartment.

"Oh, private party going on here look." Kayla winked.

"I was just leaving." Brandon said, quickly standing up.

I followed him to the apartment door and opened it. "Do you want me to watch you walk to your apartment?"

"Yes please. I'm a hot man out on my own. You never know who's going to attack me."

I stroked his cock again through his pants. "Like that you mean?"

He groaned.

"Have dinner with me tomorrow night. I'm a good cook."

"You said a good cook, right?" I winked. "I didn't mishear you?"

He laughed. "And the rest. So take some vitamins and energy drinks because I can go for a long, long time."

"I was in when you said you were cooking. But

sorry, Monday is girls' night, so it will have to be Tuesday."

"I have classes Tuesday. Can you do Wednesday?"

"I can indeed."

"My balls are going to explode before then. Give me your cell," he demanded.

I passed it to him and he punched in his number.

"I'll text you tonight. I can't finish you off in person, but I can sext."

He leaned over and kissed me again. Then he headed the few steps to his own apartment.

"Later." He said and went in and closed the door.

He wasn't kidding when he said he could sext... I was a limp puddle in bed after ten minutes.

I was so looking forward to Wednesday evening!

CHAPTER SEVEN

Tiffany

He might have invited me to dinner, but hell we both knew it was mainly about dessert. I treated myself to some brand-new underwear. My bra was light pink with a black net overlay. On the inner and outer edges the overlay was floral and in the middle it was laced up with eyelets like on a bodice. It was unusual to find a bra to suit my huge breasts that also looked sexy, but I had pulled it off. I was wearing a matching thong. After staring at the closet for what seemed like hours wondering what to wear, I eventually settled for a button through shirt dress that could be tantalizingly removed.

I kept my hair down and a little messy and wore light, fresh looking makeup. I left off the gloss. It seemed disloyal to H somehow, which was crazy given he was a one-time fuck buddy.

I left the apartment with catcalls and jeers from Kayla (mainly) and Haley, then walked the few steps outside to Brandon's apartment door. I knocked and waited. He opened the door and the smell of some kind of sauce permeated the air, making my stomach rumble.

"Chicken in white wine sauce. Sound good?"

I put a fake look of dismay on my face. "Fuck, I should have told you. I'm a vegetarian."

His face fell. "Damn. I wanted to surprise you. Never mind, I'll order takeout instead."

"I'm joking, let me in." I said. "It smells delicious."

"You're going to get spanked for that, you tease," Brandon smiled and shook his head.

"I can categorically assure you that I eat meat." I said and winked, walking through to his living room.

I was expecting a typical bachelor pad with dark tones and a lack of accessories, but the apartment was decked out in neutrals and had green accents throughout, with soft furnishings. My surprise must have showed on my face.

"I rented it as it was. I haven't had the time to furnish it myself. The only thing I brought with me was some gym equipment," he said. I followed him down the corridor and he opened a bedroom door revealing a bench press, treadmill, and some weights. His apartment was a similar layout to ours except it had only two bedrooms. He told me that his room had an en-suite and there was a separate bathroom which was just like ours.

"I'll show you the bedroom later. Let's eat." He stated and ushered me into the kitchen.

AFTER FILLING OUR STOMACHS, we moved to the couch. Brandon put the rest of the bottle of red wine and my glass on the coffee table in front of me while he cracked open another bottle of beer. He pulled my legs over toward his knees and started to massage one of my feet. I had been in heels all day while showing properties and the feel of my toes being massaged felt amazing. I groaned in pleasure.

"Fuck, that noise you're making. Want to move into the bedroom and see how many more sounds I can get out of you?"

I nodded. "Yes, please."

We walked to his room. When he opened the door, it was again not what I expected. Unlike my own room, which was full of abandoned clothing, Brandon's room was completely tidy. He had a dark wood nightstand, the top drawer of which was slightly open and crooked.

"Come here," he coaxed.

I walked over to him in my bare feet.

"How tall are you?" I asked.

"Six foot three."

"Hmm, so tall." I said. "I'm five foot seven, you make me feel like I'm so tiny."

"You won't be thinking about our height in a minute."

I smiled. "Good."

He unfastened the first of the buttons on my shirt dress, then another.

"I don't have the patience for this," he groaned in frustration and with a yank he ripped my dress open from head to toe and buttons flew everywhere.

I gasped, both with the shock and the cool feeling as the air hit my skin.

"I'll buy you a new dress." He said as his eyes raked down my body. "Fuck, you're beautiful. I can't wait to be inside you."

My pussy instantly throbbed and became slick.

Brandon stalked toward me and fisted his hand into my hair. He claimed my mouth, sucking my top lip into his own mouth, then nibbling and biting. His facial hair scraped against my mouth and upper lip and I wondered how it would feel between my legs. I felt a jolt between my thighs.

The difference between Brandon and H became clear. Night and day. Brandon was focused on my pleasure, not his own. Oh, he wanted to come, but he was intending to wait until I'd had several orgasms myself first. He backed me onto the bed and pulled off my thong, situating himself between my thighs and licking up my slit. I bucked up off the bed as his lips wrapped around and sucked hard on my little nub. He brought every nerve to life.

"Oh, Christ."

My skin erupted in goose bumps as he teased my hard nub with his tongue and alternated this with probing my pussy. His stubble brushed against my folds, adding to the sensations. I grabbed the top of his head in my hands, pushing him closer to my core as I felt my first orgasm building. I fell apart over his face, shudders erupting from me.

"Fuck, Tiff, you came so hard. I could feel you shaking against my mouth."

He dove back down and feasted on my cum. When he raised his head again, his chin was glistening with my juices. He grabbed my head and kissed me, and I tasted myself on his tongue.

"You're sweet like fucking honey. I could taste you all day."

Next, he feasted on my breasts, removing my bra and sucking hard on each peak, while his fingers pinched my clit. I felt so fucking naughty as I bucked wildly against his hand.

"Bounce my tits around. Grab them, squeeze them." I begged.

He sat astride me and pushed one of my breasts upwards. "Have you ever licked your own tits?"

"No." I blushed. It seemed so wrong to even consider it.

"Do it now. I want to watch you. I want you to finger yourself while you suck and lick your own tits." He sat back on the bed.

I sat up and rested against his headboard. Then I moved myself onto my knees and spread my thighs apart. Grabbing my left breast in my left hand, I pushed it upwards toward my mouth, leaning my neck over and licking the pink bud. I could just reach my nipple with my tongue and I flicked it. Then I placed the fingers of my right hand into my wet pussy. My juices pooled down onto the sheets making a wet patch.

I took a look at Brandon. His cock was in his hand. It looked painfully distended. All purple and enormous. He slowly rubbed his hand back and forth against his shaft. I took in his washboard abs, and I closed my eyes and imagined it was Brandon on my breast.

"No. Open your eyes." He commanded. "I want you to know it's you licking yourself and playing with your pussy."

He must have read my mind.

So I did as requested. God, what did I look like to him? My knees splayed apart as I showed him my wet, pink snatch, complete with landing strip pubes. I pushed two fingers inside me while I used my thumb to flick across my bud. I feasted on my own tit making a noise that belonged in a porno. "Mmmm."

"Talk dirty to yourself."

I juggled my tits. "Come on, baby girl, lick your tit. Oh god, oh yes." I spoke to myself out loud, then took my breast back in my mouth and nuzzled it. Then continued my dirty talk. "Oh, your fucking juices are spilling all over my fingers. Fuck me, god yes, fuck me. I wanna come so bad."

I looked around his room and my eyes fixed on

something. "Can I get up off the bed and do something?"

"As long as it's hot and makes you come like a hurricane."

I moved over to the edge of his bed where there was a narrow bedpost. I sank my cunt on it and watched as the post disappeared inside me.

"Oh fuck. I'm never going to get that vision out of my mind." Brandon groaned.

I moved myself up and down on the post, flicking my clit at the same time.

"Oh fuck, I'm coming, I'm coming Brandon. I'm going to come so hard."

I bucked and shook over the post, then lifted myself off and lay across the bed. My chest heaved with my heavy breathing.

"Fuck, that was hot."

"It's your turn." I told him. "Do you want me to suck your cock?"

"No. I want it straight inside you, filling you to the hilt." He growled. Brandon leaned over to the partly opened drawer, and extracted a condom, quickly sheathing himself and then he plunged into me. I was so wet he slid straight in. I was so damn sensitive from my recent orgasm and I was on the edge after a minute then climaxed again. Brandon rested his cock against me for a moment while I recovered. Then he slowly began to slide in and out of me, going deeper with each thrust. He pushed my thighs further apart. The top of my thighs ached I was stretched so wide. He pushed my legs up so my knees were bent and held an ankle in each hand. "Are you ready for me? I'm going to fuck you until you can't walk straight."

I nodded eagerly. The truth was, I couldn't get enough of his cock and the orgasms he was giving me. I was insatiable and craved more.

He slammed inside my walls completely filling me.

"Oh God." I screamed.

He thrust further inside me and even harder. I came up off the bed he was so rough, yet I wanted more.

"Fuck me, fuck me harder with your massive cock."

"Yeah, baby, tell me what you want."

"I want to feel you cum. I want to feel your balls tighten and you erupt."

"Won't be long, baby. You're so tight. I can't last much longer."

He quickened his pace, thrusting in and out of me. I screamed, "Yes, yes, yes."

He grunted and groaned. "Oh fuck, fuck, your tight pussy." He tightened and then flooded the condom with his cum; a loud guttural cry escaped his mouth. He grabbed me and pulled me into his arms.

"That was amazing, baby girl. I've never had a fuck like that in my life."

Brandon slipped out of me and removed the condom and headed for the bathroom. I turned over and closed my eyes. A few minutes later, he slipped into the bed behind me and spooned himself around my back as we fell asleep.

I opened my eyes and saw the bedside clock. It was just past midnight. I felt Brandon's erect cock between my ass cheeks. He rubbed himself there.

"I've never done that." I whispered. "I don't think there's any way I could take your huge cock there."

"We can work up to it," he whispered back.

His arm that rested around my front, against my belly, started to move and his fingers once again trailed a path down to my pussy. In minutes I was soaking wet again. He smeared a finger in my juices and then moved his arm around to my rear. He placed his digit against my puckered hole. I tensed. "Relax. It's only my finger."

I breathed slowly and felt myself relax. He

rubbed my wetness against my asshole and then began to push his digit inside. At first, I felt myself clench around his finger, but then as I relaxed my breathing, my asshole relaxed and his finger pushed right in.

"See, you did it. How does it feel?" He asked me.

"Fine. I feel a little naughty having something in there. What does it feel like to you?"

"I can feel your ass walls, they're kind of spongy. I want my dick inside there sometime. I need you to know that. Can I try another finger?"

"Yes."

He took his finger out and then pushed two in. Again, my body accepted it without a problem. He pulled them out and pulled me, so I was on my back half resting against his hip. The fingers of his other hand splayed against my pussy and he strummed my clit, then dipped in and out of my channel. His hand was behind me and he pushed fingers into my asshole again. "Baby, you have three in there now. I'm going to fuck you with three fingers in your ass and three fingers in your wet pussy."

"Oh yes, please."

I bucked against him as he began his ministrations. He co-ordinated the thrusts, so they happened simultaneously. My ass felt full. His fingers felt deeper than the ones in my pussy. I thrust my hips up and down, taking in all the new sensations.

"You like it up your ass, don't you?"

"Yes."

I let my imagination fly and pictured H in my cunt and Brandon in my ass. I came hard within a minute of that fantasy.

"Oh, baby. I need to fuck you again."

He moved me on top, and I moved astride him and grabbed hold of his dick, sinking it inside me. It felt so good. Again, I was soaked, and my wetness dripped onto his stomach. He trailed his fingers in it and then pushed his fingers into my mouth. "Taste yourself. That's all for me." I sucked on his fingers and then when he slipped them out, I tipped my head back. I grasped hold of my tits and as I bounced up and down on his cock. Brandon pulled my hands away. "That is a sight to see, baby; those massive tits bouncing around right in front of my eyes. I feel like I'm in a porno movie."

I smiled thinking that I'd had the same thought earlier. My thighs were beginning to burn with the effort of bouncing up and down. I needed him to coach me at the gym as well as in bed. It was okay for him and his gym, sculptured body. Jesus, I couldn't remember the last time I'd had a workout like this!

He grabbed hold of my ass cheeks, holding them apart and groaned as I continued to move. This time I circled my hips a little, so I pivoted around on him.

"Oh yeah, keep doing that. God, yeah, just like that. Don't change a thing."

I felt the pressure of my orgasm building once again and I exploded, my pussy spurting out a large amount of liquid. Fuck, I must have pissed myself a little. I hoped he wasn't offended by water sports!

He pulled out his dick and sprayed his cum all over my tits. It ran down between my breasts and onto my stomach. Brandon grabbed my hips and moved me to one side, then he leaned over the bed and grabbed his t-shirt. He wiped off my stomach and breasts and then between my legs. After that he wiped his own cock, then leaned back against the bed, a massive, satisfied grin on his face.

"I'm so sorry," I apologized, looking guilty. "I've never wet myself before during sex. I must have lost complete control."

"Baby," he gathered me into his arms. "You didn't pee, you squirted. Not many women can do that. Have you heard of it?"

"Oh my god, I did? Yeah, I've heard of it, but didn't really know what it was. Are you sure I did?"

He kissed my forehead. "You did, and I am so fucking honored that it was your first time."

"I had lots of firsts today." I told him. "First time anything went up my ass too."

"I hoped you would be up for that." He said. "I have something I bought earlier. Can I give it to you and maybe take a photo? I have a Polaroid."

"I think you should show me what you bought first."

He opened his bedside drawer again and drew out a box. Then he removed the box lid and took out something shiny. I saw that he held a silver object in his hand. He covered one end of it up with his closed fingers, but the other end had a small silver ball visible.

"What is it?" I asked.

"It's a butt plug." He explained. "I'd really like to put it in you and take a photo."

"Oh, I- I'm not sure." I said. "I don't mind trying the plug, but I don't know about the photo."

"Just two. One for us both to remember tonight. I will just take a shot of your hole wearing it and you'll see a bit of your ass cheeks. No one will see it, and no one would know it was you if they did. Please? I want to jack off while looking at it."

"You mean you have the energy for more?" My eyes widened.

"When it comes to you, it would appear I can't stop." He answered.

"Okay." I told him. "For your eyes only."

He put the ball in front of my mouth and asked me to suck on it. "Lube it up baby."

I sucked on the cold metal. Then he withdrew it. "I'll just get some extra lube."

After a minute, I felt a cold wetness as his finger teased my puckered hole, slipping some of the lube inside me.

"Bend over on all fours." He requested, and I did so.

I felt the cold of the ball against my asshole and then he pushed it slowly in. Again, I felt full.

"God, it looks so beautiful. Stay there while I take the pics." He moved from the bed and I heard a door open, which I presumed was his closet. He got back on the bed and I heard the camera shutter twice.

He pulled out the butt plug and put it back in the box and back in his drawer. We waited for the photo to appear on the film. He put on a pair of low-rise lounge pants and I visited the bathroom to clean myself up and then quickly got dressed. I noted that

I'd have to hold my dress together with my hands between here and my own bedroom.

"Thank you for tonight. I hope it's the first of many dates." Brandon whispered as he moved himself against my body and kissed me. "I really like you, Tiff, and I thought that before the amazing, mind-blowing sex."

"I had a great time too, but now I'm exhausted and need my bed, or I won't be able to work tomorrow. Keeping me up late." I pretended to scold him.

"I think actually you kept me up," he winked.

He walked me out of his room and I headed toward the door, slipping my heels onto my feet before I left.

He pushed the photo into my hand after not letting me look at it before.

"Wait until you're in your bedroom on your own." He whispered.

"Okay."

We kissed again for a while in the doorway before I backed away from him with a groan. My lips felt swollen and I ached between my legs. "I have to go. I'll see you soon, okay?"

"Yes, we'll make another date. I'll message you."

I headed back to my own apartment.

When I got in, I breathed a sigh of relief when I

realized both Kayla and Haley were in their rooms, presumably asleep. I didn't want twenty-questions at this time in the morning and my legs could barely hold me up. Actually, I was too tired to even brush my teeth and put on pjs. I placed the photo down on my bedside table, shrugged out of my dress and climbed straight under the covers in just my undies. Then I picked up the photo.

It was indeed just a photo showing the cheeks of my ass and the butt plug in between. What I hadn't seen however—as it was covered by Brandon's clenched fingers—was the end of the plug had a jeweled embellishment. Shining out of my ass was a diamond encrusted silver star.

Fancy that! A silver star. I put it down to coincidence, dropped the photo into my top drawer, and placing my head on my pillow, I fell asleep in seconds.

CHAPTER EIGHT

Tiffany

I was in love.

No, I wasn't kidding.

I was seriously, head-over-heels in love with Brandon Bailey.

The only time we had spent apart for the last few months or so had been on my Monday girls nights, and when he had classes and gym sessions to run. Other than that, we had dated and fucked. It was sheer bliss. Who would have thought when the new neighbor moved in that he would become my guy!

Certainly not me. I had an extra bounce in my step which meant I was owning it at work too. My commissions were HUGE this month.

So, why was I still thinking of three-ways?

CHAPTER NINE

H

I watched her still.

She had no idea.

She was too busy falling in love.

It's what I wanted for her. Marriage, babies, the white picket fence.

I couldn't give her that.

Anything else she desired, yes.

But, not that.

That part of me would always belong to my wife.

I could love Tiffany, though it would hurt.

But I couldn't give her the world. I already gave that to someone else.

And now they were out of reach, and my everything was still with them.

CHAPTER TEN

Tiffany

Brandon was working, and the girls were both going out. I was going to S.

I wanted to visit the place on my own. No Kayla to distract me. No one to follow me around. I intended to observe tonight. I wanted to know what happened in those rooms and I definitely wanted to see tonight's show.

I changed into a black jumpsuit with a silver chain belt, and placed silver heels on my feet. The jumpsuit had a deep V at the front, so I made sure I was secured with tit-tape. The key would look like a carefully chosen accessory. I ordered a cab, and within the hour I was back inside the club, drinking a Bellini.

The auction tonight was different. The only thing to bid for was the stage itself. A couple won the bidding and once again at one am, we gathered around to watch the show.

The man, who I pictured to be in his early fifties, came out onto the stage dressed as an aristocrat. He wore a black suit with a waistcoat. He had on a white shirt with an upturned collar and a black tie. When his partner came on dressed in a long black dress with a white pinafore over, a frilly cap-like thing on her head, I guessed these two had a serious obsession with Downton Abbey.

"I've brought your tea, Sir."

"Thank you, Mary. You look chilled. Please, take a seat by the fire."

Mary looked toward the imaginary fire and knelt in front of it.

"I am so cold, Sir. You will catch your death outside, so be sure to wrap up warm should you venture out."

"You're so kind, Mary. Come here and sit beside me in my chair. It's much more comfortable than the floor."

Yeah, come here so I can stick my cock down your throat.

Mary walked over to her Master and tried to sit in the chair on the stage but there wasn't enough room. She ended up sitting on his knee.

"I apologize Mary, you're sitting atop me in this manner has made me hard. I hope you aren't offended. It is a sign of my attraction to you."

"I'm not offended at all, Sir. I'd be very honored if you'd let me see it. I've often wondered what one looks like."

"You've never seen a phallus, Mary?"

"No, Sir."

"Well, let me show you."

Sir dropped his trousers to the floor and kicked them away. Then he pulled down his briefs and freed his member. "You may touch it, Mary."

Mary grasped his cock and stroked her hand up and down it in a very practiced manner for someone who'd supposedly never seen one before. I looked around me. People were really getting into the scene, but it wasn't doing anything for me at all, yet I carried on watching.

She put her mouth around his cock and sucked, drinking every last drop of his cum.

"Mary."

"Yes, Sir?"

"I thought you hadn't seen a man's member before, but you seemed to know how to suck my cock very well."

Mary looked downward. "Sir, the truth is I have practiced with Thomas so I knew how to satisfy you if I ever got the chance; but I swear my virtue in intact and is only for you."

"Come here, Mary, and lay across my knees with your bottom in the air. You need to lift up your dress and remove any panties."

Mary did as she was told, and her ass stuck out toward the audience.

"Do you understand you need to be punished for tricking me?"

"Yes, Sir."

"Good."

He raised his hand and brought it down sharply on her ass, striking at her white flesh. I watched as it pinked up between his repeated strikes. In between each one he rubbed across the pink, mottled flesh. Mary groaned with each further slap to her behind. Sir stopped and placed his fingers between her thighs.

"You're saturated, Mary. Someone likes a good spanking, don't they?"

My own panties had now dampened. The idea of being 'punished' by someone, I realized, turned me the hell on.

Sir pulled off Mary's cap and undid her hair, so it reached her shoulders. He held it in his hand like a ponytail and dragged her to the bed by her hair. "I'm going to fuck you now, Mary, and if I find out you've lied about being a virgin, I will fuck your ass as well."

He penetrated her hard, thrusting with all his might and Mary screamed with delight, "More, Sir, more."

He stopped, withdrew, and removed his tie.

"Strip off all of your clothes, Mary."

She did so and stood in front of him.

He put his tie around her mouth. "You will be quiet. I do not wish to raise the attention of other members of this household. This shall be our little secret, Mary."

She nodded and opened her mouth for the tie to be fastened around her.

When she was gagged, he pushed her onto the bed face down and mounted her from behind where he gave her one of the hardest poundings I'd ever seen. You could see when she came because she twitched and then tried to move up the bed away from him, but he grabbed her by the waist and held her in place until he came. He then declared her a virgin by pretending he'd seen evidence of virgin blood.

The performance was over, and people started to applaud. I was dissatisfied and walked away toward the now open doors to the other rooms.

As I walked inside, a doorman nodded to me and indicated three bowls with wristbands. My brow creased, and I looked at him with a question in my eyes.

"Madam. White is for observers. Blue is for people who are partnered. The black with silver stars are for those who would like to be approached by others."

"Thank you." I told him, and I took a white wristband and put it on.

I walked down a corridor. It reminded me of exhibits in an aquarium. Large glass windows went the entire way down the right-hand side. Behind the glass there were rooms, sectioned off with partitions that could be opened or closed. It became apparent that there could be private sex play or an entire gang-bang behind these windows.

I continued to walk down the corridor glancing in at the action, seeking something I had yet to find. Then I saw what I had come for.

A woman laid on a bed. There were two men with her. The men were both masked and dressed in black long-sleeved t-shirts with just their bottom halves nude. This room had the sectioned off area pulled across. It was a scene only for the three of them plus observers. I stood behind others who were watching and peeked over a man's shoulder as I wasn't yet comfortable with openly watching the action before me. I don't know how long I watched but I saw everything. I didn't know how this woman remained able to continue.

One fucked her mouth while the other fucked her pussy.

One fucked her pussy while the other fucked her ass.

One fucked her ass while the other fucked her mouth.

She took both of them in her mouth.

She performed oral on one then the other, a long suck for each until they masturbated themselves and came on her face.

One fingered her pussy while the other sucked her breasts.

It never seemed to end.

I was dripping wet, my juices pooled in my panties, and I needed to come so damn hard. I'd had enough of being at the back and moved forward to watch as she once again got fucked in the pussy by one man while the other one laid across her face with his cock in her mouth. No one was watching me, all eyes on the scene in front of them, so I placed my purse across my pubic area, holding it with my left hand and my right hand disappeared under the purse, rubbing across my satin dress material. Why the hell hadn't I worn a dress slit to my thigh? I flicked my finger across my clit. I knew I would come in another couple of strokes. My eyes closed, and I bit on my top lip as my orgasm washed over me. I opened my eyes a moment later. What the hell was I doing? I looked quickly around me. No one had noticed thank God. I had lost my common sense. I looked back into the window. The fucking had finished and one of the men seemed to be staring straight at me. I looked behind me but there was no one there. The man removed his mask.

It was H.

I gasped and ran down the corridor, away from the rooms and out of the club. I grabbed a cab and rushed to the safety of my own home. All the way there I scolded myself for going there. I was in love with Brandon. Why had I felt the need to go to the club?

When I got home, I felt full of guilt. Brandon was all I needed. I didn't need a club, and I didn't need a ménage. There were ways around this. I sent him a text.

Tiff: You awake?

A text came back.

B: Can be??

Tiff: I'm coming over. Make some room.

Brandon had given me a spare key after a couple of weeks as I spent so much time there. I grabbed my dildo from my bedside drawer and left my apartment and let myself into Brandon's. I crossed the corridor and headed to his room. The light from the moon and street lamps cascaded through onto the bed and I disrobed and climbed under the duvet. He turned toward me and curled me into his arms. His warm front was against my cool back.

"You need warming up." He said in a sleepy voice.

"Sorry, to wake you." I whispered.

"Don't be. I wasn't sleeping well anyway. When you're not here, I don't. I miss you."

"I miss you too."

He propped his head up on his arm against the

pillow. "So, what have you been up to tonight that kept you out so late?"

"If I tell you, promise you won't be mad."

His posture stiffened.

"It's nothing bad." I stroked down his arm, and he relaxed.

"I visited that VIP club. The one I went to with Kayla that time. It's a sex club. I was curious, so tonight I went again. See, I wanted to go alone so I could see what happened. I hope you don't mind that I went. I didn't do anything, except watch."

I felt his erection pressed against my back.

"Well, I knew you liked being fucked, but I hadn't realized you liked to watch too."

"I'm not sure I do." I confessed honestly, turning around to face him. "The first scene didn't do it for me at all. It was watching someone being fucked in their asshole and their pussy that I liked. Also, the spanking turned me on. Anyway, I brought this with me." I placed my dildo in his hand. "I figured that maybe you could fuck me in one hole and use this for another, and I could get to experience how it felt for myself."

"God, I love you." Brandon groaned. Then his posture went rigid again as he realized what he had just said.

I stroked down his cheek, leaned in, and kissed him with all I had. "I love you too, Brandon. Now fuck me so hard I can't walk."

I guess some people who professed their love for each other would follow it with a dose of tender and gentle lovemaking. I found myself pushed further up the bed while Brandon feasted on my pussy.

"You're sopping wet. Is this how you left the club?"

"No. I washed between my legs when I got home, this is all for you." I panted.

My nipples were hard as pebbles. Brandon twisted and pinched them while feasting on me. I lifted my pelvis up to his face trying to get his tongue to sink deeper into my cleft. The feeling was amazing. My breasts heaved into his hands as I writhed beneath him. As I was on the cusp of coming, he moved away from me.

"No. Don't stop." I cried.

"I'm not stopping." He grunted. "Turn over."

He slapped my ass cheek. It stung, but it felt good and as he did it, it pushed my nub against the linens. I groaned.

"You enjoyed that, didn't you?" Brandon almost growled, his voice was so low and husky.

"Yes. Do it again."

"You need to learn your lesson." He strummed my clit, taking me to the edge again and then stopped.

"That's what happens to naughty women."

"I'll be good, I promise. Please, spank me again."

"I'm going to give you five strokes and you'd better not come."

I wasn't sure I could promise this, but I said it anyway.

"I promise."

"One." Slap.

"Two." Spank.

"Three." Thwack.

"Four." Slap.

"Five." Spank

"Oh my God. I'm so close."

Brandon stuck his fingers in my mouth. "Suck on all your juices. I need you to calm down a bit, otherwise the finale won't be as good as I want it to be."

I sucked like a good girl.

"Now play with my cock. Get me ready for you."

He came to sit further up the bed. I moved myself so that I could stroke his shaft and pump him. Then I brought him over to my mouth and sucked and swirled on his immense cock.

"Christ, I can't wait any longer."

He turned me back, so I faced the bedcovers and dragged me up onto all fours, doggy style. He grabbed the dildo. Rubbing his hands through my wetness, he smeared my cum over and around my asshole and then he opened his tube of lube and had me dripping. He positioned himself at my rear entrance and pushed in.

I pushed back against him, relaxing so my puckered hole relaxed to accept his girth.

He pushed in more and we got a rhythm going until he was fucking my tight ass with long strokes.

Then he reached underneath me and pushed the dildo into my cunt.

I felt so full from his cock and the dildo. He pushed the dildo in to match his thrusts. I lifted one of my hands off the bed and grabbed and pinched at my own nipples. I had never felt anything like it in my entire life. It was exhilarating having both holes fucked at once. I hungered for more, for the feel of an extra cock instead of the dildo. In my mind it was two men who were fucking me. I screamed out my orgasm as it claimed my entire body. My mind, body, and soul were flying through the air, and as I came down, I was so breathless I felt a small amount of panic that I had gone too far and might have half killed myself during sex. As I came back to myself, I felt Brandon tighten, and he came all over my ass cheek—the one he'd spanked—and I felt him rub his cum into my skin.

We didn't need any more words that night.

He gathered me up in his arms and we slept until his alarm went off.

CHAPTER ELEVEN

H

I sent a text the next morning.

She needs more.

It took an hour, by which time I wondered if I was being ignored, but then a reply came back.

So much more. She's ready.

I called Green's and explained that there was a problem at the condo I was in the process of purchasing and that I would need Miss Harris to meet me, so we could solve it. They must have sent her a message right away.

Tiffany: There is no problem at that condo is there? What do you want?

H: I want to talk to you about something. It has to be in person.

Tiffany: I won't tell anyone what I saw at the club. I would be grateful if you would extend me the same courtesy.

H: The Club is entirely confidential. What happens in the club...

Tiffany: Stays in the club, right? Well, I was just curious about the rooms. I have a boyfriend. I'm happy.

H: I'm glad you're happy. I just need to talk to you about something. I promise I won't touch you.

Tiffany: Okay.

H: Unless you beg me to...

CHAPTER TWELVE

Tiffany

This time I made sure I was dressed in a dark black pant suit. I added ankle boots. Beneath the jacket of the suit, I had a pale pink blouse, but the jacket was wrap style and mostly covered me apart from a flash of pink at the neck. I straightened my hair and left it down, trying to look as conservative and professional as I could. I didn't want H thinking I was there for him to fuck again. I was with Brandon now.

As I entered the condo lobby, my mind flashed back to the time in the apartment. Why had he not wanted a repeat performance though? Had I not been good enough? Was that it? Why I was here? Because he wanted to give me some pointers, so I could satisfy Brandon better? Who the fuck knew. The best thing I could do was go to the apartment.

When I got to the correct floor and walked to the condo door, it was already unlocked. I walked through to the room and found H standing at the window. He was dressed in jeans and a tee. My heart leaped, and my pussy got wet. Traitorous heart. Traitorous core. He looked so much younger, dressed casually. He ran a hand through his blond hair.

"Tiffany. Thank you for coming." His voice was thick and husky.

I nodded. At a loss for words.

"So, I guess you're wondering why you're here?"

I swallowed, trying to make my throat wet enough to speak.

"Just tell me what you need, so I can go. I have a lot of work to do and then I'm meeting Brandon."

"Ah, yes. Mr. Bailey. The one you're in love with." H looked back out of the window. "But he's not enough, is he? Not on his own. You need more."

My eyes narrowed. "What are you talking about?"

"The club. Last night. I watched you watching

the three of us. I saw you make yourself come. You liked thinking of two men fucking you, didn't you?"

"No. I didn't do any such thing. You're imagining things."

"So why, when you got home, did you go to see Mr. Bailey and let him fuck you with his cock and a dildo to imagine what it's like then?"

My jaw dropped, my heart plummeted to the floor, and I stared at H.

"Are you spying on me? What the fuck is going on?"

"No." Brandon replied, as he walked out of the bedroom and came toward me. "I told him myself."

I stood stock still, rooted to the spot. How could Brandon be here at the apartment, in the same room as H? Oh my god, was it all a set up?

I placed a hand on my hip. "Someone better tell me what the fuck is going on here."

The men looked at each other.

"Do you know what? Forget it." I shouted, and I ran from the room. I couldn't wait for the elevator. I headed for the stairs and ran down them as fast as my heeled shoes would let me until I reached the foyer. As I moved toward the exit I was stopped by Matthew, H's driver.

"Miss Harris. Please, wait a moment."

"Matthew, I can't. I need to leave."

"I've got this now, Matthew, thank you."

I tilted my head back in frustration at H's voice. His strong hand was now on my arm and I was powerless to move unless I wanted to make a scene in front of the many guests in the lobby.

"Please, Tiffany. Come to the bar and let me explain. It's not what you think it is."

"So it's not a set up? You didn't put Brandon in that apartment?"

He sighed.

"That's what I thought." My eyes teared up. "I told him I loved him. What a fucking fool I am."

"No, you're not. Please, come to the bar."

I nodded and walked alongside him. To be honest, I felt so foolish and devastated I wanted to hide, and my legs felt like they wouldn't hold me up any longer.

"Two brandies please." H requested from the bartender. I didn't protest, instead I asked him to make it three.

I walked past H and found a dark corner of the bar area, where I took a seat. H sat down at the side of me. He was too close. His knee was alongside mine. The bartender brought over our drinks and placed them on the table. I drank one straight down, choking as the alcohol burned my throat and tears stung my eyes.

When I recovered myself, I narrowed my eyes at H. "I'm listening."

"It's no secret that I want you, Tiffany. However, I felt that maybe my attraction for you was too much."

"Too much for whom?"

"For me." H took a sip of his brandy.

"I lost my wife twelve years ago. A brain tumor. She was carrying our son at the time. I lost the love of my life and the family I should have had."

I covered my mouth with my hand, while I stared at the man at my side who was now slumped in his chair, looking down at his hands.

I took a moment to compose myself. "H, I'm so sorry."

He rubbed the heel of his palm on his chest and in a flat, monotone voice said, "I won't allow myself to commit again to a woman. Veronica was my life, my world, and that's the position where she will always stay." He drank the rest of his brandy and motioned for the bartender to bring another. "You had the right idea, to order more than one." A slight smile crossed his face. The man at my side then brought himself up to a straighter position and returned to the H I knew.

"So, I have sexual partners, but I have never loved anyone else. But then I met you."

"We only fucked once. You're staying true to your wife."

"That's just it though." He replied. "For the first time since I lost her, I wanted more."

I gasped.

"I do want more." He added. "Tiff, I want you in my bed on a regular basis. I want to take you to nice places. I want to love you."

I took a large swig of my brandy because for a moment I felt I might faint.

"But you would want more. You would want marriage. A family. I can't give you those things. So, I sent Brandon to live in the apartment."

I jolted in my seat.

He held up his hand. "Stay. Let me explain."

I sat while I waited for the words that I expected would tear my life apart.

"Brandon works at a gym I own. He was looking for a place to live. I asked him to flirt with you, maybe take you out a couple times. I wanted you to be distracted from our rendezvous in the condo. To have some fun. But then he told me he'd fallen in love with you. And I watched as you fell in love with him. I was happy to step back. He can give you what I can't."

I closed my eyes. My relationship with Brandon wasn't fake. Thank god for that. A deceitful start that I had to think about, but our love for each other was genuine. I could have cried with relief, but the man in front of me wasn't going to get to see my emotions for another man.

"Then, I watched you at the club. The first time, when you saw the auction and the ménage on stage you looked shocked. Then you came back by yourself and you watched me, though you didn't know I was under the mask. You got off on it, on seeing two men with one woman. You went home and took the dildo to Brandon. I had told him, if he was enough, I would walk away. Back right off. But if you craved more, I would step up."

"What do you mean?"

"You love Brandon. You can have a family life with Brandon. But we are willing to offer you more. Brandon is a good man and he sees that he is not enough for you sexually."

My mind tried its best to process his words and the fact they were true. It was devastating to hear the facts out loud, but yes, sexually I craved more. It might be that a one-time experience would be enough. I didn't know. But I desperately wanted to know how it felt to have two men at once.

"So, what now?" I asked.

"Now, Brandon comes down to talk to you. You can either leave with him, or..."

"We come back to the apartment."

H smiled. "It's been a pleasure to meet you, Tiffany Harris. I hope to see you again, but if not, I wish you all the best for your future." He lifted my hand, kissed the skin next to my knuckles and then rose from his seat and walked away.

What the fuck just happened? And, what did I do?

I FELT like a girl waiting for a blind date to show up. I was so nervous as I sat looking for Brandon. He walked around the corner and I saw his head rise searching for me. I waved to him and he smiled. I loved his smile. My stomach settled because of that reassuring smile.

"What are we drinking?" He asked.

"Brandy, but I've had two already."

"Third time lucky," he winked and motioned for a bartender.

When we had our drinks in front of us, Brandon took a deep breath. "I'm so sorry, Tiff, for not being completely honest with you. I wanted to tell you so many times about how I had been asked to flirt with you, but then I fell for you anyway."

"So, why didn't you?"

"Because I was scared you would walk away. Kick me to the curb. I didn't want that. I don't want that. Tiff, I want us to be together always. I want you to wear my ring and have my kids. Do you feel the same way? Or have I damaged us forever by taking a chance that you want more sexual freedom?"

"You haven't damaged us forever. It was a shock that's all. A shock that's still there but having the edges dulled by brandy."

"And I haven't scared you talking about commitment?"

"No. Because I feel the same way. When you know, you know, right?"

"Well, I'm glad you feel that way," he replied. Then he dropped to one knee and opened a box.

"Tiffany Harris. Please would you do me the honor of becoming my wife?"

My fingers splayed across my mouth and my body shook. "Oh my god. Oh my god. Yes." I squealed. He placed the ring on my finger—a diamond solitaire—and I jumped into his arms almost knocking him over.

"How did you know my ring size?"

"You sleep like the dead, Tiff. I measured it then."

I pushed him with my now diamond adorned hand. "It's a good thing you're gorgeous."

He pushed a piece of my hair back behind my ear. "There's no rush on a wedding, okay? Whenever you want. I know we have been only dating a few months."

"Excuse me."

We looked up, having forgotten that anyone else existed, to see the bartender standing beside us. "Sorry, but we saw the proposal and on behalf of the Brighton Condominium and Club, we would like to offer you our heartfelt congratulations."

We noticed there was a small crowd of people standing around us and as we took the bottle of champagne, they gave us an ovation.

"I think we should take this back to the room, don't you, Mrs. Bailey-to-be? That's if you're ready to have all your wildest desires met?"

I hesitated and sucked on the left side of my bottom lip.

"Tiffany, if you don't want to do this, you can say

no. I'll be happy to tell Henry to leave. If we start it and you've had enough, same thing. If we commit to this relationship, it's going to be once every two weeks, okay? At any point, you say the word and the arrangement is finished."

I nodded. "Okay. Listen, I want you to know that I find Henry attractive obviously, but I don't know him. I don't love him. I love you."

"Well, I'm comfortable enough with my manhood that you can like him a little bit." Brandon laughed. "Now take my hand, fiancée, and let's not keep the man waiting any longer or he'll think we left."

He led me to the elevator, and we went back up to the apartment.

When we walked back through the door, H was back looking out of the window and he turned to stare at us when we came through.

Brandon nodded to him. "We're ready."

I blushed. How did this work? I felt so dirty saying I would fuck two men at once.

H spotted my nervousness. "Tiffany, Brandon and I discussed how we would do this if you agreed, so all you have to do is let yourself go fully. We will lead you through the first time."

"Don't forget, you can stop this at any time." Brandon's voice was full of concern.

"All you need to remember, Tiffany, is that ultimately we're here to worship your body. This is all for you." H whispered. I glanced from Brandon to H and it became clear to me. They were here to meet my deepest, darkest desires and no one but these two knew about them. I felt the tension leave my shoulders. I undid my jacket and then my blouse and I threw them on the back of the couch. Finally, I took my shoes off my feet and shimmied out of my pants, so I was left in a light-pink sequined bra and a matching lacy G-string.

"Let's move it to the bedroom." H's voice was cultured and smooth.

My mouth dropped open when I walked in. Although he had yet to complete the sale, he had already changed the furniture. There was a huge king-sized bed in the room. H went to stand by the window and Brandon walked up to me. He leaned in and kissed me, capturing my tongue with his own. He slid a strap of my bra down my arm, then the other and backed me onto the bed. Once I was lying back with Brandon at one side of me, he pulled down my bra to reveal my huge tits and sucked on them. Then he turned to H. "There's plenty to share."

H joined us and knelt at the other side of me on the bed. He swirled his tongue around my nipple. My tits were being sucked on by two men at once. I swore my pussy would sing if it could. The sensations were almost too much for me to bear and I moaned and gasped and begged for more. They removed my bra and panties and their eyes explored every inch of me.

I expected to be treated like a sex slave, so I was surprised when instead I was almost worshipped by them. They trailed fingers over my skin, caressing every part of me. H grazed his fingertips across my clit and I arched upwards. Brandon showed me two of his fingers and then pushed them inside me. They fingered and played with me. At one point, H added a light tapping pressure to my bud, and it tormented me to the edge of an orgasm. I cried out for release. H moved over, and Brandon spread my legs apart, parted my folds and licked my pussy. H once again added his fingertips to my nub. They kept a steady rhythm until I surrendered my body to its crescendo and exploded all over their face and fingers. I opened my eyes, and a thrill went through me as I saw two men both by my pussy.

"You're too dressed." I complained. "Take all your clothes off."

They both smiled and walked to opposite ends of the room where they stripped. Jesus Christ. Two huge cocks. I might need vaginoplasty after this.

"Shuffle to the end of the bed, Tiff," Brandon said in a commanding voice.

I did as he asked. The men stood to each side of me.

"Suck our cocks." Brandon added.

I took Brandon's cock into my mouth and as I sucked on it, I grasped H's dick and began to pump it with my hand. Then I swapped. I did this for a long time, enjoying comparing one and then the other. I asked if I could hold them together and they nodded. I grasped them between my fists and stretched my mouth open as wide as I could to take in both cocks at once. The edges of my mouth felt as if they were going to rip apart, but I sucked for all I was worth, while I tickled up their shafts with my fingers. Drool ran down the sides of my mouth.

When they withdrew, my jaw ached.

"We're going to fuck you hard. Any preference as to who takes your pussy and who claims your ass?" Brandon asked.

"Surprise me." I said.

They asked me to kneel. Brandon came to the front of me. "As H has not yet experienced the delights of your asshole, I'm letting him play there first."

"How thoughtful." I giggled.

Brandon knelt in front of me and cupped my mound. "Ah, sopping wet as always. Ready and willing for my dick."

He pressed his girth against my cleft and pushed inside, filling me.

I groaned in response.

"You're dying to feel what it's like with two cocks inside you, aren't you?" Brandon added. "To see how it compares to my cock and the dildo."

H was at the side of us. He lubed up his pulsing shaft and then placed himself behind me. His dick nudged at my asshole.

"Relax. Make it easy for me."

He pushed forward, and his cock sank in me an inch at a time. I was stretched so much by Brandon's cock and now H's at the same time. This was not something I would want all the time—to some extent it was strange and uncomfortable—but I guessed like anything you had to get used to it. Then they both started to move. H had one hand holding my hip, and the other wrapped around my front and he pinched my nipple. Brandon had one hand on my hip and the other fingered my pussy.

"Are you okay Tiff?" H asked with concern. "Do you want us to stop?"

"Fuck no. Fuck me, please." I begged enjoying every thrust.

They picked up the pace, thrusting inside but being gentle. My pussy was soaked with my juices and I squirmed under Brandon's fingers as my orgasm built. I screamed so hard when I came that I was scared they were going to call security. H and Brandon pulled out and jacked themselves off to their own orgasms. They sprayed their cum all over my front and back. Brandon picked up a couple of towels from the end of the bed and threw one to H as he wiped himself and then me.

"We thought we would go gentle the first time. What did you think?"

I smiled and looked at them both with devotion. "That was amazing. I could never have estimated what two men at once felt like."

"Let's hit the shower." H said, "and then we can rest."

The water in the large walk-in shower cascaded down over our naked bodies. H grabbed a sponge and soaped it up. Once again, I was the filling between a Brandon and H sandwich. I was lathered up and my body washed while Brandon got the shampoo and washed and then conditioned my hair.

I noted that they were both rock hard again.

I dropped to my knees and took Brandon in my mouth. He groaned and tipped his head back. H stroked his shaft as he watched me give oral pleasure to Brandon. Brandon came into the stream of water and I watched his cum as it swirled away down the drain. He moved me nearer to H and nodded his head. H backed me against the wall and grabbing his cock, he thrust inside me. While he fucked me, I kept my eyes on Brandon. It was so fucking hot being fucked by one man while another watched. H's thrusts meant I was repeatedly jostled against the wall and I imagined someone watching us now, seeing what we had all been doing together and I begged Brandon, "Suck my clit."

He lowered himself to his knees and from the side of me he licked my clit, biting and sucking it. Against the plunging of H's cock, it was too much, and I came, squirting my juices all over Brandon's face and H's cock.

"Did you see that, H? Our little Princess likes to squirt."

"I did." He replied. "I'm very impressed."

I felt strangely proud, as if these were my

teachers and I was the star pupil. Maybe that was a role play idea for another time?!

H once again soaped up a sponge and washed between my legs and then his cock. Brandon also washed himself and then we stepped out and wrapped up in bath towels. We made our way over to the massive bed and once dried, we climbed under the duvet. I was cradled between two taut bodies and it was total bliss. I completely surrendered and fell asleep.

When I awoke, I saw that H was up and getting dressed.

"Hey," I said to him quietly.

"Hey." He nodded to the bedside table. "A key for you."

"But you haven't completed the sale yet."

"Money buys anything, Tiffany, and I have a lot of it."

He stroked my cheek. "I hope to see you again sometime." He picked up my hand and studied the ring. "It's beautiful. Congratulations. I hope you'll be very happy together."

"We will be." I told him.

He walked out of the bedroom door and I heard the click of the outside apartment door as he left. I curled back up to Brandon and fell back to sleep.

CHAPTER THIRTEEN

Tiffany

I kept everything that had just happened to myself until the Monday evening, though I was desperate to tell the girls about my new experiences. Kayla came home with Chinese food for us all and as usual we opened some wine. After the meal, at the point where we usually choose a movie, I finally filled them in on all my adventures.

"Oh my god. I am so jealous of you right now." Kayla pouted. "I didn't even know I wanted a ménage, but I do now."

Haley sighed. "I have enough trouble with one

man and one penis, never mind double the trouble. Are you sure it's not going to get messy, Tiff?"

"Well, we can only see what happens." I replied. "If Brandon starts to find it difficult, I'll stop it. My love for him is stronger than my need for an extra cock. They make plenty of realistic dildos these days."

"So why not do that?" Haley asked.

"Because it doesn't come with an amazing chest with rock hard abs." I smiled.

I hadn't worn my engagement ring yet, so I went into my purse. "I have something else to show you. Just a minute."

I brought my hand out when my sparkling diamond was in place.

"Oh my fucking god." Haley squealed.

"Haley Martin! Scrub your mouth." Kayla mocked. "Tiff, it's Brandon you're marrying right? Not both of them or just their cocks." She added.

"Yes," I rolled my eyes. "Brandon asked me to marry him and I said yes. I know it's fast, but we agreed we don't need to rush to get married, but hey, we're madly in love."

The girls flung their arms around me for a group hug.

"So, the other thing," I told them. "I'll be moving

out and into Brandon's apartment. The good news is I will only be a few steps away. We can still have our Mondays if that's okay with you?"

I looked at Haley. "I'll give you notice okay and pay whatever rent you need to cover the place while you find another tenant."

"Actually," Kayla interrupted. "I'm doing really well at work and if possible, could I pay Tiff's share and have her room? It will mean I get the bathroom to myself and I can use the extra bedroom as a walk-in closet.

"That would be great. I would be nervous to get a new tenant. What if we didn't like them?" Haley stated. "That's settled then."

We toasted my engagement and all the new arrangements, and then Kayla chose *Bride Wars* and spent the movie debating how much of a Bridezilla I would turn into.

CHAPTER FOURTEEN

One year later...

Tiffany

I WAS NOW Mrs. Brandon Bailey. Mrs. Tiffany Bailey. We had gotten married a few weeks earlier and had just returned from a honeymoon in the Caribbean.

Last night I had caught up with the girls. Haley's love life was unfortunately no better, and Kayla was getting ready to go visit her stepfather, as he said he needed to speak to her about her mom. Apparently, she had caused chaos again. Kayla joked about it all, but I could see it was getting her down.

For part of our engagement present, Kayla had given me her key to S. She said it was my place with H owning it, and she didn't ever want me looking over my shoulder if I visited, thinking she might be there watching me. Well, her actual words had been, 'If I saw you with your snatch out I'd vomit', but I learned to speak fluent Kayla a long time ago.

Of course we saw each other at work too, but we rarely got time to chat there, always out trying to earn more commission.

Anyway, tonight, Brandon and I had received a special invitation from H to the club. It was our wedding present from him. He had said we could dress however we liked because he had ordered costumes for us. I was already excited. We had been in our regular ménage for just over a year now and it worked beautifully, once every two weeks. H and I were extremely fond of each other. I would go so far as to say we loved each other, but we weren't *in* love. My confidence in the three-way had grown, and I thought H intended to capitalize on that tonight. We would see if I was right...

.   .   .

THE AUCTION WAS ABOUT to begin. The emcee took the microphone and explained that a private bid had been entered for this evening and so the stage was sold. Then a gentleman walked up to our table and asked us to follow him. We walked through a side door, down a hall, and into a room that resembled a fitting room in a store. There were shelves of different clothes, but looking at them closely, they were costumes of different kinds.

"If you could stay in here to change, Mrs. Bailey, your outfit for the evening is in the white box." He nodded toward a large, rectangular shaped white box which was wrapped in a black ribbon. "I will be back for you in about ten minutes, please enjoy the refreshments. Mr. Bailey, if you could follow me next door."

Brandon kissed me on the mouth. "I'll see you soon."

I took a drink and then lifted up the box. Walking over to the chaise longue in the corner of the room, I took a seat, then untied the bow and removed the lid. Carefully, I pulled back white tissue paper to reveal a black, wet-look PVC bustier and matching panties. There was also a pair of what must have been six-inch stilettos in black patent. I would be lucky if I could walk down the corridor in them.

H totally had a thing for sex with a woman in high heels. There was a note in the box asking for me to tie my hair back in a ponytail and a black band in the box to secure it. I walked over to a full-length mirror in the corner of the room. Having a fitness instructor husband agreed with me. My body was tanned from our honeymoon and toned from all the swimming we had done, plus the gym sessions I attended a couple times each week, hitching a ride in with the hubby. It was hard to stay away when the instructor was so hot!

Finally ready, I poured myself a glass of the champagne on ice, and nibbled on a couple of the strawberries on the silver platter at the side. I didn't intend to eat much here as I was waiting for my main course on the stage.

There was a knock at the door. "Mrs. Bailey, are you ready?"

"I am."

The gentleman came back in. To his credit he treated me as if I was fully dressed and asked me to follow him again. I thought we would be getting Brandon from his room as well, but we didn't. I walked very slowly and carefully down the corridor in the stupidly high heels and finally I was asked to climb a few steps to where there was a side door. Apparently, that would take me onto the stage.

"What about my husband?"

"The men are already on stage, Mrs. Bailey." He pointed to a hook at the side of the door. "When your performance is finished, I will be waiting here with this robe for you and will escort you to the aftercare room."

"Aftercare?"

"Yes, it has a shower, so you can freshen up. I will move your clothes there while you are on stage."

"Thank you...?"

"Mitchell, Mrs. Bailey. My apologies for not introducing myself earlier."

"Thank you, Mitchell. I'm Tiffany."

He held open the door for me and I walked onto the stage.

THE STAGE WAS BRIGHT, but the audience were in muted tones of darkness, with the bar backlit at the rear. I thought I would be overwhelmed at everyone watching, but it was hard to actually make out any of the faces. Anyway, I didn't care. This was what I had been asking for, for a month or so now. To make it onto the stage at S and perform in front of everyone. I had asked for a smorgasbord of my favorite fantasies and that was my present, our wedding present, from H.

On the stage was a bed. On the bed were red satin sheets, all the better to slip and slide across. The ultimate in a girl's wet dream, yet far too impractical to actually make it onto my bed at home. Lying on that bed was my husband. He had a leather mask across his eyes and was wearing a leather thong. Sitting on a chair at the left-hand side of the bed was H, dressed in a suit.

"You're late. Our entertainment was booked for midnight. What sort of a whore are you that doesn't keep to time? If you charge by the hour, you need to arrive on the hour." H barked.

"I'm so sorry. It won't happen again." I said in a quiet voice.

"Hmm, maybe we'll send you back. Unless you can state why we shouldn't?"

I had no clue as to what would happen on the stage, so I made it up as I went along. "Because I'll do anything."

"Anything? What do you think, B?" He turned to Brandon.

Brandon sat up and leered at my body.

"She's hot, let's keep her. I have an idea for later."

"Well, she must be punished for arriving late." H walked over to a drawer and brought out what appeared from the black fronds to be a flogger. I stared at his hand. The handle was glass and sparkled under the light. It was a dildo, a glass dildo. He handed the flogger to Brandon.

"Okay, we tossed a coin and B is the first to get to play with you. I'm going to sit back over here and watch. You'd better be worth it."

Brandon moved off the bed slowly and his eyes raked over my body like a predator. "Remove your panties." He commanded. "Then sit on the edge of the bed."

I walked over to the bed and dropped and stepped out of my panties. Brandon picked them up and threw them to H. "Something for you to play with while I play with her."

H lifted the panties up to his nose and sniffed the hem which I knew was already soaked with my juices. "She smells divine, as you'll know when you're tonguing her pussy."

Brandon knelt on the floor in front of me and pushed my thighs wide apart. He sat to one side so my glistening, wet core was on display to the crowd watching. "So wet," he growled. "But your punishment first."

He held the flogger in his right hand and gently whipped it over my pussy. It tickled, and my clit responded with a jolt like an electric shock. As he repeated the motion, I tried to arch my wet pussy up toward it.

"Keep your ass on the bed. If you do that again your punishment will only get worse." I was dying to know what that worse punishment would be, so I raised my hips up again.

Brandon stopped what he was doing, reached and grabbed my ponytail and dragged me onto my feet. "I warned you." Now lie across my knees.

I positioned myself so my ass was high in the air. Brandon brought the flogger down on my ass cheek but did it hard this time, so it stung. I whimpered. "Good girl, keep quiet and take your punishment." He smacked me another four times. I could feel heat radiating through my ass cheek.

"I think that's enough. Now it's time for my own pleasure. Lower my thong and suck my cock."

I dropped back onto my knees. Brandon stood in front of me. We were sideways on stage to the audience, so they could see our actions. Brandon's eleven-inch cock protruded hard as a rock and I took him into my mouth and expertly gave him head. I tongued the underside of his shaft, pumped the base with my hand and sucked hard. He fucked my mouth hard, holding my hair by my ponytail once more. My head bobbed up and down with the motions of the blow job he was receiving. "I'm going to come and you're going to swallow it all." His seed spilled into my mouth and I swallowed and then licked around my lips. He withdrew his cock and patted me on top of my head. "Well, you are a good girl after all. I think I may allow you to come now."

He picked the flogger back up and sitting back on the edge of the bed he put his fist on the bed so that the glass dildo was standing straight up. "You can do all the work. Fuck it."

I moved onto my knees on the bed, so I was positioned just over the dildo. Then I sank myself down onto it. It was cold, and it made me shiver as it entered my pussy. The combination of the cold and the fact it was so hard made my pussy clench around it. I could care less that I had an audience. All I searched for right then was my orgasm, because I was so fucking wet and horny.

"Do not close your eyes. Watch yourself fuck it." Brandon demanded.

My eyes looked down and I watched myself come up off the dildo. It was dripping with my cum. In fact, my cum pooled onto Brandon's hand as he held the base of the dildo. "Please may I touch my breasts?" I asked.

"You may."

I pushed a hand down the right cup of my bustier and I pinched and tweaked my nipple as I continued to fuck the dildo. My breath came out in short, sharp pants as I pumped up and down on the glass cock. "Oh, god, ooooooooohhh." I jerked as my pussy pulsated. Brandon pulled the glass cock away and my legs buckled, and I sank onto the bed.

Brandon got up and walked over to H, handing him the glass dildo. "Your turn. I want to watch for a while."

H slowly moved out of the chair and slipped off his suit jacket. He stood in front of me, unbuttoned his shirt, removed it and tossed it on the floor. Then he demanded that I unfastened his pants and free his cock. He wasn't wearing underwear. Another giant cock was in front of me and I wanted to snack on it.

"Get on all fours on the bed so your ass is pointing at me," he ordered.

Now my puckered ass was on display to the whole audience.

"Time to introduce your new friend to another receptive hole."

He pushed the dildo into my tight asshole and

once I was relaxed around it, he thrust it firmly into my ass. God, it felt good. He fisted his cock with his free hand while he hammered my ass. I could hear the noise of him doing it. The noise stopped and my bustier was unfastened at the back. It fell off around my waist. My breasts swung like gigantic pendulums.

"I'm ready." H informed Brandon.

H removed the dildo and threw it onto the stage floor.

He grabbed my hand and pulled me with him toward the floor at the very front of the stage.

"So, B, what was your hot idea?" He asked.

"A spit-roast." He answered.

I was guided onto all fours and H positioned his cock in front of my mouth. Brandon was at my rear.

"We're all going to come together." H informed me.

I tried to imagine what this looked like to the audience. I was sideways, completely naked with my huge tits hanging down. When they fucked me they would swing around. I had one massive cock teasing my lips with pre-cum being rubbed into them and another was teasing the entrance of my pussy.

"Ready?" H asked Brandon.

"Yes."

And they entered me. With a tandem rhythm they worked their cocks in deeper. I deep throated H while my pussy gushed around my husband's cock. I felt my breasts, freed from their constraints, bouncing around. I looked up at H and he watched my breasts. Our performance was polished, and I yielded to the pleasure that coursed through my body. H was the first to reach his pinnacle. His balls retreated, his cock tightened, and he exploded all over my face. His hot, sticky cum ran down my cheeks and onto my chin. Then Brandon pinched my clit and that sent me over the edge. I shuddered around his dick as I felt his own cum spill inside me. A few moments later after we gained control, we all stood up and faced the stage. Cocks still dripped, and cum still ran down my chin and from my pussy. Our most intimate selves were on display in front of a hundred or so people. They broke out into applause. The lights rose, and I saw that so many of them were half dressed themselves. Fingers were in pussies; cocks were in mouths, pussies and asses. The doors opened at the edges of the club and patrons made their way over, ready to continue the party for many more hours.

But we were finished for now. Maybe forever. I didn't know. The arrangement had been a fantasy lived out, but now a reality was starting. Brandon and I were planning a family, and we had agreed we would finish on a high. H had just accepted our notice. He didn't think we would return to the scene afterward. He thought it was out of my system. H did say the door might be open if we came back later, but added that his own life was moving on and he was seeking fresh adventures.

Our finale then could not have been any finer, played out on the stage in front of a captive audience.

The curtains dropped. H took my hand, dropped a kiss there and walked away.

As I walked behind him, I was handed my robe and helped down so I didn't fall down the stairs, still in those goddamn heels. "Damn, woman, I thought I only had to carry you over the threshold, not down club hallways too." Brandon threw me over his shoulder and spanked my ass as we headed toward the aftercare room.

THE END

Double Delight continues with SUBMIT – Kayla's story.

Read on for a sneak peek...

Author note: You can read the continuation of H's story in *The Billionaire and the Virgin*, though for your ultimate reading experience finish the Double Delight series before moving onto the Billionaires.

SUBMIT
Double Delight Book 2

Kayla

It was time to visit Daniel, my stepfather. He had been messaging me for a couple weeks now, saying he needed to catch me up on some news from my mom. I had delayed visiting saying I needed to give notice to take vacation time from Green's, the realtors I worked for. He was bound to know I was bullshitting him; he had never been a dumbass. As I threw clothes into my suitcase, Haley, my roommate hovered in the doorway.

"I'll to miss you, Kay. It's going to be so weird being on my own in the apartment."

"Hey, it's only two weeks, Haley. You can spend the time masturbating away as I won't be here to listen to any rude noises. You can have a good scream."

She rolled her eyes. Haley was used to my ways as we had lived together a while now. Up until a year ago, there had been three of us, but our other friend, Tiff, now lived next door with her husband, Brandon. I had taken over her share of the apartment, meaning I had two good-sized bedrooms and my own bathroom. We still saw Tiff every Monday when we had our girls night where we ate good food, watched a movie and gossiped.

I had never told them much about my stepfather though. Or about my mom. They knew she had paraded me through a stream of stepdaddy's as she chased money. My mom couldn't live her life without wealth, and I had been an unfortunate incident for her. Her relationship—if you could call it that—with my father, had been the catalyst for all the drama that came after. He had left her penniless, and she had sworn it would never happen again.

Out of all my stepfather's, Daniel, who I had met when I was seventeen, had been the only decent one.

The only one who had realized I existed, beyond being a hanger on. He had told me I always had a place at his home, and even after my mother had worked her way through most of his wealth and moved onto Chuck, the stepdad that came after, he still reminded me I could stay anytime. I had never fully worked out my mom's relationship with Daniel. They had never seemed hooked on each other like she had with some of them. Her public displays of affection with one or two had made me feel nauseous. Largely through my life, I had kept my head down and done the best I could with my education, given the fact I was never at one school for very long before she had us on the move again. Once I turned eighteen, she had moved on once more and this time she told me she was done raising me and I was on my own.

It wasn't the shock it could have been. Like I said she had been absent most of my life anyway. I graduated and eventually started at Green's where I made my good friends and never looked back. I'd had a couple boyfriends but no one special. The girls were used to my cocky manner about guys, but to be truthful I was more talk and no action if you get me. I'd not had much experience, though I was no virgin. I was kind of jealous of my friend, Tiff. She had been enjoying a ménage for the last year. That woman walked around the whole time like she still had a cock up her pussy. I swear she always wore a shit-eating grin. Jealous, me? You better believe I was.

Anyhow, I couldn't put off visiting Daniel any longer as he had said my mom had been causing chaos again, and he needed to update me. I had hoped she wasn't hanging around for his money again as he had recently recovered his wealth, having had some of his art bought by a prestigious gallery. When I had first met him—when he and my mom hooked up—he was the owner of a string of tattoo parlors. He had secretly painted on canvas, using the talent that had drawn designs on clients, until he had finally got the guts up to show them to someone. They'd loved his work and taken a couple pictures to try in a gallery where they had been bought by a collector the same day. He now had a new profession which was great because my mom had nearly caused him to go bankrupt with his tattoo business.

I hadn't stayed at Daniel's much. Instead, a schoolfriend's mom had practically let me move in there, knowing my background with my own mom. No, I hadn't stayed at Daniel's very often for a good reason.

I had always had a huge crush on my stepdad.

There was no way I could have lived with him and my mom. If they had kissed, I would have wanted to punch something. I knew that was stupid. Girls got crushes all the time. But Daniel was something else. He was ten years younger than my mom and had been twenty-eight when I first met him—eleven years my senior. He had dark shaggy hair back then and the darkest eyes. When he smiled, he always looked sexy and goofy at the same time. His face all kinda crinkled up. He had these really plump cheeks when he smiled. I had always wanted to reach out and touch them. I was sure that whenever he spoke, heat rose in my cheeks. I guess that was when I had started to become the brash kind of Kayla because I hadn't wanted to appear all young and innocent around him. Thing was, I always felt he was trying to save me, you know? Always telling me I had a home with him, even after my mom almost ruined him. He had gotten this look in his eye like he hadn't wanted me to lose touch and even though I had tried to cut contact with him over the following years he had never given up. Still texted, called, sent me birthday and Christmas cards, and checks I never cashed. When I visited I would do it on the way somewhere else and not stay long because I couldn't. Being too close to him killed me. But now I had to go, and he had told me I would need to stay awhile—at least a few days—so somehow I would have to work through this crush I had. I was twenty-four now. It had been six years since my mom had hitched a ride with her next victim. I had never seen or heard from her again, yet now she had done something that affected Daniel and me once more.

Zipping up my case, I turned to the doorway. I had been so lost in thought, Haley had left. I spent some time with her before I drove to Daniel's. She was my best friend, and I was gonna miss her while I was gone.

The drive to Port Jeff was less than a couple hours which made my lack of visits there even lamer I guessed. I swung into the large driveway of Daniel's colonial. He was so lucky to have not lost this amazing property. His four bed, four bathroom home in Harbor Hills looked out over the waterfront and had its own private beach. I exited my car, leaving it in front of the double garage and walked to the front door where I rang the bell. After a couple minutes the door opened and Daniel stood there.

He looked as hot as ever and I felt my cheeks burn again. Why was I so goddamn sensitive around him? His face broke out into his signature smile and he stepped forward and embraced me in his arms.

The heat from his body enveloped me. I didn't want to move, but he then outstretched those strong arms and looked me over.

"Hey there, Kayla. It's good to see you. You look well."

I half smiled at him, feeling uncomfortable.

"Shoot, ignore my manners leaving you out here on the porch, come inside. You need help with your luggage?"

"Please. There's a case in the trunk."

"I'll grab that and then I'll park your car in the garage. We'll take your luggage to your room and then I'll fix us a drink, okay?"

"Okay," I replied.

I hovered in the hallway while I waited, taking in the vastness of the space. Every time I came here, the place took my breath away. He hadn't decorated the place and the realtor in me saw the potential of the property that had yet to be unleashed. The hall had a central staircase leading up to a landing from which all the other rooms veered off. It was a little old fashioned to me with its wooden moldings. It cried out for a modern makeover. If it were mine, it would be fabulous.

"Okay, let's get your things in your room." Daniel had reappeared with my case. I grabbed my duffel from the floor and followed him up the stairs.

This wasn't good. He was wearing jeans, and they hugged his ass as he climbed the stairs. I wanted to reach out and feel his ass cheeks, see if they were as peachy as they appeared. His biceps bulged as he carried my case up the stairs. I felt between my thighs get wet. For fuck's sake, he was only walking!

We headed a little way down the hall to my old room. He pushed open the door. It was exactly how I had left it, or rather, how my mom had decorated it. The room was ocean blue—everywhere. With its frilly curtains and bedding, it hurt my eyes to look at it. Daniel caught the grimace on my face.

"Maybe we could decorate while you're here? Make it more your own?"

"Maybe. Though I'm not planning on staying too long, you know. My life's back in Brooklyn and I need to return there as soon as I can."

Daniel nodded. He looked a little disappointed, and that made me feel bad.

"Though I guess it wouldn't hurt to do a little makeover, given the hideous paint colors in here."

"Great." Another smile broke out on his face. "It would be good to get the house looking a little more modern. I need to make the most of having a hot realtor in the house."

At that, my face burned so hard I thought I might need a fire extinguisher.

Daniel ran a hand through that still shaggy brown hair. "Christ, Kayla. I meant hot as in good at your job. Jesus, I'm an idiot."

"It's fine." I waved my hand in front of my face. "I knew what you meant, and I am really great at my job." I needed to get sassy Kayla back as soon as possible. That's how I was. Confident, and not afraid to speak my mind. "I've seen enough of this room for now. How about you fix me that drink and we sit out on the deck?"

"Sure," Daniel answered.

I needed him out of my bedroom.

We walked back down the stairs, entering the hallway and then walked off to the right, through his vast living room with its dark leather chairs and huge TV, and out into the back yard. There was an acre of lawn out there, complete with a heated swimming pool at the rear of the lawn and a pool house. I had spent a lot of time in the pool house when I had visited when my mom lived here. It had been a place to escape, with its comfy couches and two separate rooms, one with a queen sized bed, the other a bathroom. Right now, I could see it was all opened up. At the left hand side was the living room area with its large screen television against the far wall. To the right was a kitchen with all mod cons. It was perfect for hot summer evenings, lazing by the pool and eating a barbeque. We had never done that there. We had never been enough of a family to eat together, never mind relaxed together.

"I know you always kinda liked staying out there." Daniel nodded towards the pool house. "But it's better for this trip that you stay in the house."

He excused himself to go fix the coffee, and I took a seat on the swing seat out on the decking. There were two separate seats on it so I didn't have to sit too close to Daniel. He came out with two steaming hot mugs of coffee and placed each one on a side table at the side of the swing seat before taking his own seat.

"So, what's she done this time?" I cut to the chase. No point in waiting around to find out what chaos my mom had caused.

Daniel turned to me. "She's shacked up with a film producer this time. They got married a month ago."

It was good to see my mom hadn't changed. Still after the men with untold riches and still keeping her only child out of her life. Not that I would have attended the wedding anyway, but hey it would have been cool to know my own mom was getting hitched again.

"So how does that impact on us? Are they making a film about her life and they want us to star in it?" I joked.

Daniel sighed.

"Ah, nothing so amusing."

"Her husband has a son. By all accounts, he's always been a little rebellious. Excluded from school; that kind of thing. His mother died when he was eight. His father excused his behavior, right up until he met your mom."

"Figures."

"He threw him out just over two weeks ago. Parker—that's his name—went through your mom's belongings and found my address, so he headed here to find you. He thinks he can get you to reason with your mom. I've tried to explain but he won't listen to me. I said I would invite you over and we could all talk. See if there was anything we could do. I said he needed to let you explain your relationship with your mom and that you hadn't had it easy yourself."

"So, where's the little brat so I can put him straight?"

Daniel's lips curved at the corners as if he knew something I didn't, which of course would be the case, seeing as he had already met this son who had been excluded from school.

"I told him to wait in his room. I'll call him now."

"Wait! In his room? He's living here?"

"Yeah. I felt bad for him. He has no one. So I told him he could stay here until he got back on his feet. I kinda think he needs a father figure."

I shook my head. "Daniel Scott's home for stray kids. You can't save us all, you know? Sometimes parents are just a waste of space."

"Yeah, my own was like that, so I guess it hits a nerve when I see it someplace else. Anyway, I'm thirty-five. I'm too young to be your dad or his dad. I know you always considered me as a stepfather, Kayla, but your mom and I were never married, so I wasn't really."

The door banged as Tom Hardy walked through it. Well, he looked like Tom, dark hair shaved close to his head, doe eyes and a wide pout to his mouth. Obviously some employee of Daniel's. He needed to watch his manners. He was acting like he owned the place.

"So sweet, listening to the old family reunion, so I thought I would come join in." He held out a muscled arm. This guy was stacked and seriously worked out. I figured he could lift me with just one of those arms.

Standing up, I took his hand, looking toward Daniel for clues, then back at the Tom Hardy lookalike.

"I'm Kayla."

"Aww, hello little... well... what should I call you? Your mommy is married to my daddy, so... stepsister?"

I stepped back. "What the heck?" I turned to Daniel. "This is Parker?"

I was expecting a boy recently excluded from school. This guy was not that young.

"Yes. Parker, meet Kayla. Kayla, Parker."

Parker grabbed my hand and shook it. A little too firmly. I felt uncomfortable as my first thought had been how sexy the hired help was. Now I found out he was kinda my stepbrother.

"I'm sorry," I said, flustered. "I was expecting someone a little younger."

"I'm twenty-one, so I'm not that old." He replied. "How about you?"

"Twenty-four."

"Well, now that those pleasantries are out of the way, I need you to come with me back to Los

Angeles to get your whore of a mother away from my father," he sneered.

I sighed. "If only life were that simple."

"Are you kidding me? It is that simple. We go back home. You tell my pop her history with men. He kicks her out. Job done."

"My mom hasn't wanted anything to do with me for the last six years, so if you think I would get anywhere near her, you're sadly mistaken."

"Well, you need to try. I'm on the outs here. She's bleeding him dry. That's my inheritance we're talking about."

"Oh, it's great to see that it's your pops you're missing." I sneered. "I've about had it with all you money-oriented bastards."

"You can't be doing too bad. Dan says you live in New York."

"I live in Brooklyn. I have a share in a rented apartment. I work round the goddamn clock to meet my rent. Don't come here playing the victim because it doesn't work with me. Do you want a nice life? Go out and earn one. I won't be helping you with your daddy issues."

I turned to Daniel. "Thanks for the coffee. I'm gonna head back up to my room and unpack. Maybe lie down for a bit. I'm feeling a headache coming on."

"Okay, Kayla." I could see in Daniel's gaze that he wanted to say more but couldn't.

"Well, I'm gonna hit the pool. I'm feeling a little heated." Parker walked off down the deck.

"I'm sorry, Kayla." Daniel's mouth was down-turned, his shoulders slumped.

"You have nothing to be sorry about." I reminded him. "I'm sorry that your relationship with my mom brought these problems to your door.

"We should talk about that sometime. My relationship with your mom."

"There's no need."

"I think there is, Kayla, because I doubt it was what you thought it was."

I nodded my head and walked back into the house. My head was already buzzing with meeting Parker and being reminded of my mom's behavior. I didn't need riddles from Daniel accompanying it.

ROMANCE IN NYC: Double Delight

Sold
Submit
Share

ROMANCE IN NYC: The Billionaires

The Billionaire and the Virgin
The Billionaire and the Bartender
The Billionaire and the Assistant

ROMANCE IN NYC: Forbidden Bosses

Abandon

Exception

Confession

ABOUT ANGEL

Angel Devlin is the contemporary romance pen-name of paranormal rom com and suspense writer, Andie M. Long.
She lives in Sheffield with her partner, son, and a gorgeous whippet called Bella.

www.ingramcontent.com/pod-product-compliance
Lightning Source LLC
Chambersburg PA
CBHW022213050726
47590CB00002B/771